"I've had time to **Sam said.**

"You're tall, but not too tall, and have nice curves, so you'll be a stunner pregnant."

"Ugh," Seton said, "don't talk about it."

"Why?" Sam looked at her. "I just meant that you'd be very beautiful carrying a baby, Seton. And I'm willing to make that happen."

"How?" she asked. "Didn't you say that our marriage would be in name only?"

"I'm flexible." Sam grinned at her, and Seton's heart jumped.

"Flexible?"

"Sure. See how hard I'm trying to make this agreement work?"

"I wasn't aware we were negotiating."

Dear Reader,

As the youngest, and the Callahan brother who "came later", after their parents had disappeared, Sam Callahan always knew he was different. Little did he know just how much he would stand out among his brothers—as an instant father to four adorable babies! Seton McKinley dishes out one surprise after another for the rascal cowboy, but Sam's going to do what he has to do to keep her for his own…and keep his new family together!

I hope you enjoy the fifth book in the Callahan Cowboys series. There's nothing better than watching a goodhearted man win the woman he loves. And as spring begins to melt away winter in most parts of the world, it's my fond wish that Sam and Seton's story will warm your heart.

All my best,

Tina Leonard

www.tinaleonard.com

www.facebook.com/tinaleonardbooks

Cowboy Sam's Quadruplets

TINA LEONARD

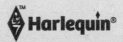

TORONTO NEW YORK LONDON
AMSTERDAM PARIS SYDNEY HAMBURG
STOCKHOLM ATHENS TOKYO MILAN MADRID
PRAGUE WARSAW BUDAPEST AUCKLAND

Recycling programs
for this product may
not exist in your area.

ISBN-13: 978-0-373-75397-0

COWBOY SAM'S QUADRUPLETS

Copyright © 2012 by Tina Leonard

This edition published by arrangement with Harlequin Books S.A.

For questions and comments about the quality of this book please contact us at Customer_eCare@Harlequin.ca

® and TM are trademarks of the publisher. Trademarks indicated with ® are registered in the United States Patent and Trademark Office, the Canadian Trade Marks Office and in other countries.

www.Harlequin.com

Printed in U.S.A.

ABOUT THE AUTHOR

Tina Leonard is a bestselling author of more than forty projects, including a popular thirteen-book miniseries for Harlequin American Romance. Her books have made the Waldenbooks, Ingram and Nielsen BookScan bestseller lists. Tina feels she has been blessed with a fertile imagination and quick typing skills, excellent editors and a family who loves her career. Born on a military base, she lived in many states before eventually marrying the boy who did her crayon printing for her in the first grade. Tina believes happy endings are a wonderful part of a good life. You can visit her at www.tinaleonard.com.

Books by Tina Leonard

HARLEQUIN AMERICAN ROMANCE

†Cowboys by the Dozen
*The Tulips Saloon
**The Morgan Men
‡Callahan Cowboys

Special thanks are absolutely owed to
Margaret Carney (St. Margaret, in my mind)
for helping make Sam's story a much better book.

There are many other wonderful folks in my writing
life, all of whom are owed gratitude. At the top of
the list are my patient editor, Kathleen Scheibling,
the magical cast of dozens at Harlequin who
unstintingly shape the final product, my family
who are simply my rock, and the readers who have
my sincere thanks for supporting my work with
such amazing generosity and enthusiasm.
I am quite blessed.

Chapter One

"Sam came later."
—Jonas Callahan, remembering the arrival of a baby
brother after their parents had "gone to heaven."

"I have a proposition for you," Sam Callahan said as he sat down in Seton McKinley's office in the Diablo, New Mexico, courthouse. "A proposal, actually."

Seton looked at Sam as he lounged in the brand-new leather chair she had situated in front of her brand-new pine desk. It hadn't been an easy decision to return to Diablo and hang out her shingle. Private investigator work in Washington, D.C., had been lucrative.

She didn't expect to make a whole lot of money in Diablo, but that wasn't the primary reason she'd returned. The primary reason was across from her, hunky and completely unaware of how he made her heart race.

At the word *proposition,* Seton's senses had gone on full alert. "Are you aware that the Callahans have quite the reputation for your propositions, proposals and plots? And I wouldn't necessarily call it a good one."

The handsome cowboy smiled at her, unperturbed. Their relationship over the past couple of years had been what Seton thought of as "friendly adversarial," with a touch of romantic longing on her side, though she hadn't breathed a word to anyone about her crush on the cowboy.

"Reputation isn't something that concerns me," Sam said, his tone easy.

Seton wasn't surprised. "Before you share your proposal, be warned that I won't do any work for you that involves Bode Jenkins. Or the Jenkins family in general."

Sam's grin widened the deep clefts around his mouth. "I'm not worried about Jenkins these days. He's been pretty quiet since my brother married his daughter, Julie."

"I spend quite a bit of time with Mr. Jenkins. I'm fond of him," Seton said, just to let Sam know she felt his comment bordered on disrespectful to the Jenkins family.

He shrugged. "Your problem, not mine, beautiful."

She frowned, studying the cowboy, from his dark, wavy hair to his slanted cheekbones. He looked like a Native American in a chalk portrait she'd seen in an art gallery. *Lawyers shouldn't be so handsome,* she thought. *It masks the devil in them, fools the eye like a mirage.*

If there was one thing she'd learned from spending time at Rancho Diablo, it was that the Callahans played for their own team, and everyone else could get bent.

"I've got a meeting in twenty minutes," Seton said. "Why are you here, Sam?"

He gazed at her in silence for a moment, during which Seton felt as if he was trying to decide if he could trust her. Or thinking how he might manipulate her into doing whatever it was he had on his mind. She waited, tapping a pencil on the notepad in front of her with some impatience.

"I don't really know who I am," Sam said, his voice soft and husky.

Seton blinked. "Most people feel that way sometimes, don't you think?"

He shook his head. "No, I *really* don't know who I am."

She put the pencil down and leaned back. Potential clients sat in the leather chairs, the only expensive elements in her new office. She had a wooden swivel chair, which was hard and kept her uncomfortable enough to focus. She looked into Sam's navy blue eyes and saw that he was serious.

Very strange for him, because he had a tendency to be the footloose charmer of the family. "You're Sam Callahan. Last of six brothers. Family lawyer and head of the legal team hired to defend Rancho Diablo from a takeover by the state of New Mexico."

"By Bode Jenkins," Sam said.

"It's *New Mexico v. Callahan,*" Seton reminded him. "You have four married brothers, and one older brother who calls my sister, Sabrina, occasionally. I'm not sure why. She's not, either. Jonas seems to be quite the chatterer since she moved to D.C."

"Jonas likes to keep tabs on everyone. He's weird that way."

"Anyway, that's who you are." Seton folded her hands on the desk. "Your aunt Fiona and uncle Burke moved back to Ireland last year. You have one of the largest ranches in all New Mexico. You rarely date, although the ladies in town would love to show you a good time. And you claim to be lazy."

"I am." Sam brightened. "That's my favorite trait. I would describe myself as having a laid-back personality. It's very important for a man to be relaxed when he's only twenty-eight. I was twenty-six when the whole lawsuit thing started."

Seton sighed. "I don't have a couch for you to lie on if you're looking for a therapy session, Sam. And I'm not really interested in learning more of your history than I already know." She cast an eye over him, realizing he probably wasn't completely aware of his physical attributes. A dark brown cowboy hat had been thrown on the chair next to the one he occupied. His jeans weren't dress, but standard Wranglers. Under a black leather jacket, a black T-shirt stretched across his chest—a T-shirt that appeared to be inside out. If he took off his jacket, she'd be able to tell.

"So?" she pressed.

"My laziness is probably a good place to start." His dark blue eyes twinkled. "I'd like to hire you in the spirit of laziness."

She shook her head. "I can already tell I should refuse."

"You haven't even heard what I want to hire you for," Sam said. "There's no conflict, I swear."

"There's a conflict anytime a Callahan is involved." Seton sat up. "I wouldn't be comfortable working for you, considering my relationship to the Jenkinses."

"An unfortunate relationship, considering that Bode is a slimy dog," Sam said. "But I can overlook some of your flaws."

Seton stared at him. "I don't want to work for you."

He waved a hand, dismissing her objection. "At least hear me out. You might like what I'm offering you."

"I doubt it." She sighed, then leaned back. "But go on. Five minutes."

"Back to not knowing who I am," Sam continued. "I think it's important for children to know these things."

"You want me to look up information on your parents?" Seton asked. "Won't your aunt Fiona tell you everything you want to know? She was your guardian since you and your brothers were very young, right?"

Sam shook his head. "I'm not so worried about me at the moment," he said. "I'll figure myself out one day."

"Okay," Seton said. "What do you want me to do then?"

Sam's expression turned serious, which made him look even more handsome, if possible. It was annoying. "I'd like to hire you to be my wife," he stated. "Although not in the traditional sense."

Seton held back a gasp. "I'm sorry. Not that I expected anything about this conversation to be normal or usual—"

"I'm sure you're aware," Sam interrupted—just like a Callahan, "that my aunt has the ranch divided among the six of us. We get our portions when we marry."

"Yes, I've heard of Fiona's wild plan to put enough wives and babies on Rancho Diablo to keep it from being taken over." Seton frowned. "It's unorthodox."

"Maybe," Sam said, "but it's working."

She looked at him. "The only thing that's kept the ranch in your family is your legal expertise." Seton reconsidered her words. "Some call it your legal maneuvers. I've even heard it referenced as shystering and sleight of hand."

"That Bode," Sam said, shaking his head. "He's such a die-hard fan of mine."

"Anyway," she said, "was that your proposal? Because I have no intention of being involved in one of the famous Callahan plots." She glanced at her watch. "My next appointment should be here any moment."

"We'll worry about that when your victim arrives," Sam said. "I'm offering you the chance to marry into one of the greatest families around. We're all really nice, contrary to what you hear from ol' Toady Stinkens. But here's the catch, which may be a problem for you. You won't have a shot at becoming a mother, which is probably important at your age." He winked at her. "I don't want children. I don't even want the ranch, honestly. I could make that confession to my family, but they wouldn't believe it, nor accept it, anyway." Sam shrugged. "I've spent years fighting for it, because they asked me to. At one time I even let my brothers talk me into being the fall guy for ownership of the ranch, which I would have then turned over to them. I would have been a puppet owner," Sam said, sounding pretty happy about being the figurehead winner of Fiona's race-to-marriage-and-munchkins.

After a deep breath, he continued. "But control isn't my thing. I'd rather slide away from the responsibility, if you know what I mean. A wife like you would make everyone think I was falling in with the plan. Except I wouldn't be." His eyes glinted mischievously. "After a while, when the lawsuit is settled and my brothers are in full lockdown mode at the ranch, you and I will quietly divorce. I plan to take off to Alaska and do some fly-fishing. Then again, I've got a yen to see the Amazon rain forest. There's so much I want to do," Sam said, his voice thoughtful, "and none of it involves a wife, and definitely not children. As I say, that may be a problem for you, since your biological clock is probably set on high alert."

Seton debated taking off her black patent high heeled pump and stabbing the crazy cowboy with it, deciding it wasn't worth ruining the only pair of pretty shoes she had. "I'll pass. And I think the shameful way you refer to Mr. Jenkins hardly speaks well of your maturity. Toady Stinkens, indeed."

Sam laughed, clearly amused. "Think about it," he said, rising. He grinned and put his hat on. "Of course, we would draw up a contract negotiating the assets you'd receive from such a transaction. Our marriage would be, after all, merely a business agreement."

Seton stared at him, astounded. All the other Callahan brothers had romanced their women like princes of yore. They'd practically thrown themselves at their lady of choice, not content until they'd won her over with great fanfare and a wedding at Rancho Diablo. The brides had all worn the infamous and stunning magic wedding dress, and the wives still glowed, as if marriage to a Callahan was the best thing next to breathing air and drinking water.

"Are you insane? Certifiably insane?" she demanded, reconsidering using her high heel to deliver his just deserts.

"No," Sam said, "just lazy, like I said." He grinned the famous Callahan smile that made ladies swoon. "Think about it, Nancy Drew. Let me know if you change your mind."

"I won't," Seton said. "You can bet your boots on that, Counselor."

"It's a good offer. Probably the best one you'll ever get." He winked again.

"Like the offer you made Mr. Jenkins recently? That if he dropped the lawsuit you wouldn't sue him for his land and every last dime he had?"

"Aw," Sam said, walking to the door, "I was trying to go easy on the old dog. I'd considered bringing up charges for bribery, misuse of taxpayer funds, et cetera, et cetera. There were about twenty charges I could have brought, none of them frivolous, and some with certain jail time attached. But at the end of the day, I decided to give the old fart a break." Sam tipped his hat to her. "I have a kind and generous soul."

He walked out, whistling as he went down the hall. Seton moved to the window, watching him amble across the street to Banger's Bait and Tackle. Several bachelorettes accosted him, and Sam put his arm around them all. They moved as a group into the restaurant, like an amoeba that grew as it moved.

"The most annoying man on the planet," Seton muttered. She locked her office door—there was no appointment, of course; she didn't have any scheduled for the entire week—and took an aspirin. Then she sank into her wooden chair, looked around her bare office and wondered if she'd made a terrible mistake returning to Diablo to see if there was anything between Sam and her.

"Take off to Alaska," Seton said, disgusted, and closed her eyes. "More like slither off."

If that was the famous Callahan idea of romance, she wanted no part of it.

"YOU HAVE TO UNDERSTAND the Callahans," Corinne Abernathy said two hours later, when Seton had sufficiently gotten over her desire to go after Sam and tell him what he could do with his stupid "proposal." "Sam especially is an unusual case, because he came last. Youngest children are always different. He didn't mean to offend you, Seton. In his mind, and with a man's limited scope, he was being efficient."

Seton sat ramrod-straight on her aunt's flowered sofa and tried not to get steamed all over again. "He's a male chauvinist, and maybe odd."

Corinne laughed, her blue eyes serene behind her polka-dotted spectacles. "One might say that about all the Callahans. They're wired differently, I suppose."

"That's no excuse." Seton gratefully accepted a cup of tea from her aunt. "What am I supposed to do with a proposal like that? I was so surprised I couldn't even throw him out on his ear, as I would have if I'd been thinking more clearly."

"Well," Corinne said, sitting on the divan across from her and putting a tray of tiny cookies on the coffee table. "I'd call his bluff."

Seton stared at her. "You don't mean accept his lunatic offer?"

She shrugged. "He's a renegade lawyer, Seton, and coincidentally, a very good man from a very good family. And you're in love with him. What do you have to lose by playing along?"

"I never said I was in love with Sam. I said—"

Her aunt waved a hand. "Seton, I may not know you as well as I know my own daughter, but I do know what a woman in love looks like. And I knew you loved Sam Callahan when you came back to Diablo. Why else would a woman return to a one-stoplight town to open up a gumshoe office?"

"I don't know. But I do intend to find out." She

looked at her aunt, who was nibbling at a pink-frosted cookie. "He wasn't the only reason I came home. I like spending time with you, too."

"Oh, I know." Corinne's eyes sparkled. "It's just gravy that's there's an adorable man here you've got your eye on."

"I should have resisted my curiosity."

Her aunt sipped her tea. "Have you ever thought that it's a bit strange he made his offer to you? There are lots of ladies in Diablo who'd jump at the chance to say I do to Sam."

Seton looked at her. "I simply figured I was the new face in town. Sam strikes me as being somewhat opportunistic."

Corinne laughed. "He's testing you, Seton."

"For what?"

"Your interest level," her aunt said calmly. "Play it out awhile. See what happens. What have you got to lose? You'll find out if you're actually in love with Sam, and he'll get what he's hoping for, which is to convince himself *he's* not going to fall in love."

Seton blinked. "Why would he want that?"

"Because he doesn't think he belongs," Corinne said. "He said as much to you with the whole 'I don't know who I am' thing. It was sort of a confession—and a glimpse into his tortured soul."

"Really?" She wrinkled her nose. "I just thought he was being dramatic so I'd feel sorry for him."

Corinne smiled. "He wasn't asking for your pity, he was asking for a snap wedding."

"Well, he's not going to get what he wants."

Her aunt's brows rose. "Don't you want to get married?"

"Yes, but not now. And probably not to him." Seton thought about children and wondered why Sam Callahan didn't want any. She did—just as he'd said. "You have to remember I've been married before, Aunt Corinne. It fell apart when I had an ectopic pregnancy and lost a fallopian tube. When I have another life partner, I'd like him to be committed to having children. Sam made it plain that he isn't in father mode. And I still think he might be odd."

"They're all a little different, as I say. But in a good way, Seton, if you have the courage to walk a different path. I've known their aunt for many years, ever since she and Burke came to Diablo, and I can honestly say that family is salt of the earth. If you think you might be in love with Sam, you could do worse, honey."

"I don't know." Seton shook her head and stood. "Thanks for letting me stay here until I find a place, Aunt Corinne."

"It's a pleasure to have you. You go upstairs and think over your options, dear. I'm sure the just-right solution will come to you."

Seton went upstairs to call her sister, who had once lived with the Callahans. Sabrina would certainly tell her to stay clear of Sam, which any sane woman would surely do.

Except for the single women in town who'd been hanging all over him as he'd gone into Banger's today. Seton frowned and picked up the phone.

"YOU'RE AN IDIOT," Jonas Callahan told his youngest brother. "Seton is never going to go for a dumb proposal like *that*." He laughed, throwing his head back, then flipped the burgers on the grill. "When you said you weren't going to be a sap and fall all over a woman like our brothers did, you went so far the other way it'll be a miracle if Seton ever speaks to you again. Ha, ha, ha."

Sam rolled his eyes and sucked on his longneck beer without much interest. "Well, she didn't exactly run screaming from the idea." Seton hadn't looked thrilled, either. Maybe more murderous than anything. "She's such a professional I figured the professional approach was best."

"You were protecting your own hide." Jonas grinned at him. "Your own emotions. That woman is so radioactively hot and major-league intelligent that she doesn't have to put up with a bozo marriage proposal." He waved the metal spatula. "Good money says she never speaks to you again."

Sam nodded and took another swig. "Probably not," he said cheerfully.

His brother eyed him. "Wait a minute. That's why you did it, you loser."

He raised a brow. "Did what?"

"Went the marriage-proposal-for-dummies route. You wanted her to turn you down! Then you could go on wheezing about all the existential loose ends in your life."

Sam sniffed. "Have another beer, Jonas. One of us isn't tight enough."

"I'm serious. You wanted Seton to think you're an idiot, which you are, but you wanted her good and convinced. So she'd turn down your proposal. And then you'd be off the hook with the only woman you've had eyes for in two years!" Jonas crowed. "You big chicken!"

Sam scratched his neck, leaned back against the

picnic table and looked up at the evening sky. "It's a beautiful March night. You shouldn't keep howling at the moon, Jonas. Only crazy people do that."

His brother snorted. "I'm not crazy. You are."

"Yeah, well." Sam emptied his beer and tossed the bottle in the trash before grabbing another one out of the cooler. "What will you do when it's your turn to propose to a woman? At least *I* did it. You, I notice, make calls to a Washington, D.C., number and somehow never get off the mark."

"I'm just keeping up with Sabrina." Jonas slapped a burger down in front of Sam. "I told Corinne I'd check on her niece from time to time."

"You didn't *check* on her sister, Seton."

"Well," Jonas said, "I was under the misapprehension that you also knew how to dial a phone, bro."

Sam bit into the burger, noting that it was done, as always, to perfection. "I don't think we need to hire a cook, Jonas. You cook acceptably. I'm not complaining." He ladled on some salsa and some avocado and kept eating, happy to needle his brother between bites.

"Back to Seton," Jonas said, "you might want to sweeten your offer. No woman consents to a hands-off marriage, so you're going to have to force yourself to be a little romantic, as much as it hurts you. Or she's going to think you're plain weird. Which you are, but right now, she's wondering if you're weird or just a hard-hearted lawyer. Neither scenario is good for your chances."

Sam licked his fingers. "Seton's independent enough to appreciate the clinical, no-strings-attached approach. And it doesn't matter, because either way, I'd be off the hook with the marriage thing. No harm, no foul, is what

I say. We're not in love, no hearts will be broken, and Seton will get a nice payday. By the looks of her office, she could use a financial lotto."

"Sure," Jonas said, "let me know how it works out, bro. And I'll keep your secret, only because it's so crazy no one would believe me if I told them what you've done." He sat down to eat his own burger, after shooting his brother one last incredulous glance.

"I expect Seton will give me her answer very soon. And then you'll be the last one left, Jonas. The last bachelor at Rancho Diablo."

Sam almost felt sorry for his eldest brother. Jonas wasn't getting any younger—or smarter.

At least I know what I'm doing.

He had a plan, and he was sticking to it.

Chapter Two

A week later, Sam decided Seton was the slowest woman ever when it came to accepting a marriage proposal. So he invited himself into her office and gave her his most winning grin, the one he reserved for sticky judges.

She glared at him. "No."

Her reluctance surprised him. "Did you even consider it?"

Seton shook her head. Today her blond hair was twisted up on her head in a businesslike braid thing, and while he thought it looked good on her, he liked her hair best loose and straight. She wore a blue suit and a continual frown, so he relaxed in the chair and pondered his next angle.

"I didn't consider your proposal," Seton said. "I figured you'd be over it once the crazy wore off."

"I never have crazy moments." Sam crossed a boot over his knee and pressed his fingertips together. "My offer was based entirely on careful planning and sound logic. You need me and I need you."

Her light brown brows winged together. "How do I need you?"

"Don't you want to get married?" Sam couldn't help doubting her happy-spinster stance.

"I've been married." Seton got up and shoved some manila folders into a nearby filing cabinet. He admired her long legs and delicate feet, tucked into navy blue pumps, and the curve of her fanny under the knee-length skirt.

"I'm sorry," he said, his attention completely shot as he tore his gaze from Seton's delectable rear view. "Did you say you'd been married?"

"Mmm." She sat back down and stared at him, her eyes clear and matter-of-fact. "It's not an experience I'm pining to repeat, to be honest." She picked up a lone file folder on her desk, consulted it for a moment, then tapped for a few moments on the keys of her open laptop. "But after your business offer—"

"Proposal."

She looked at him again. "One can't really call that a proposal, Sam. It was all about business. *Your* business. The only thing you forgot was something for the other party. Negotiations tend to be short-lived when one party wants something and the other wants nothing."

"I mentioned there would be financial compensation, Seton," Sam said.

"Which sounds unethical."

"Oh," he said. "I see where you're coming from."

"I doubt it." Her tone was cool as she returned her gaze to the computer screen. "But in the spirit of friendship, and I suppose we'll have to have some kind of friendship since we're both living in Diablo, I did a little searching for you."

"I don't need you to search out a wife for me," Sam

said, feeling crusty. "I'm not going to make my offer to just any woman. Thanks."

"About your parents," Seton said, shooting him a glare. "Forget about the marriage bit—that horse isn't going to run. Let's focus on the real problem you have, which is that you said you didn't know who you are."

He raised a hand. "I'm not in a hurry to find out."

"It seemed like that was your big hang-up when you were in here the other day. Your real reason for wanting a wife. An anchor, if you will."

Sam shrugged. "Wrong theory, Miss Marple. Anyway, you're going out of order. I came here to talk about marriage. Not myself."

"I'm not accepting your proposal."

Well, wasn't she just the most stubborn little thing? It was almost cute. There was something between them, even if she didn't care to notice it. Sam supposed a woman didn't decide to become a detective without some good ol' ornery in her makeup. Seton was so no-nonsense she probably scared most men.

Sam liked a challenge, and the more pretzel-like the chase, the better. He figured he'd be a pretty poor lawyer if he didn't crave a good knuckle-cracking challenge. He leaned his chin on his fingertips and tried to think where he was going wrong here. It was really important that Seton say yes. Marriage would solve everything for him. He wouldn't be the last one on the range. What man wanted to cross the finish line last? *He* sure as hell didn't. Jonas would be much better at being the family wallflower. Frankly, things were awkward now at family gatherings. There were all his brothers, their wives, their children—and him and Jonas. Like a date, or an old pair of doting uncles who couldn't measure up to what a woman needed in life. He hated being Sam the Single Callahan.

Besides, he had a yen for Seton.

He sighed. "So what did you find, Snoopy?"

"Snoopy?"

"Did I ask you to snoop around in my life? I asked you to marry me, not go on a hunt for clues." Sam couldn't help the grieved tone in his voice. "I guess that would come with the territory, though."

"What territory?" Seton shot him an annoyed glance of her own.

"Marrying a private investigator. You'd always be digging around, looking for stuff. Frankly, I don't have that many fossils to unearth." He spread his hands wide. "I'm a pretty simple guy, actually. I just want a companion. I want to get married so Fiona won't fix me up."

"She's in Ireland."

"Don't make the mistake of thinking that matters," Sam said darkly. "Fiona would send over a mail-order bride if she could find one who could finesse me to the altar."

"Maybe she should," Seton said sweetly. "Since all you want is a name on a piece of paper."

He looked at her. "All right. I get that you're not impressed. But what would you do in my place? Just think about it for a moment."

Seton shook her head. "Maybe this will help you. There are no records of your parents in Diablo. Not their births, obviously. But there are no records of their deaths."

"Did I ask?" Sam snapped.

She narrowed her gaze on him. "If you don't want to know what I found, I certainly won't reveal it, Sam."

"I'm not paying for it." He leaned back again, noting that his gut was all churned up.

She shrugged. "I didn't ask you for anything."

This was true. He chafed at the reminder that only he seemed to want something. He admired her independence, even while it annoyed him. "I don't appreciate you being nosy," he said.

She turned off her computer. "I apologize."

"You were trying to help me find myself," Sam said, "but see, I don't want to be found."

She looked at him. Confronted with knowing that his past was a very empty one made him irritable. If there were no death records in this county, then his parents had died somewhere else. Fiona had never been clear on that. They'd always known they should have asked her, but Sam more than anyone didn't want to know. Because once he asked, he was going to find out that his parents weren't the same as his brothers'. There was no other reason for Jonas to remember that Sam had come "later"—after their parents had died.

He stood. "You're right. We wouldn't suit. I'm looking for a simplifier in my life. You wouldn't be simple."

She blinked. "Sam, I apologize for offending you. I just searched public records. It wasn't like it took me more than five minutes to look through records that are open to anyone—"

He shoved his hat on his head. "It's fine. Don't worry about it. Thanks, though."

He departed, and Seton thought she'd never seen Sam move so quickly. She sighed. It was going to be awkward now every time they ran into each other in town. He hadn't wanted to know anything about his life—had run from learning anything at all.

How did a woman accept a man's offer when he claimed he didn't know who he was?

Seton turned back to the case she'd accepted yesterday, involving a woman who thought her sister was siphoning off her funds by using her identity. Identity theft wasn't as interesting as missing persons work, but Sam didn't want to be found, and this job paid, so Seton sent Sam out of her mind.

She had to stop thinking about how very much she'd actually considered saying yes to his outrageous proposal.

"Maybe Aunt Corinne had a point," Sabrina said when Seton called her that night. "Maybe you should have played it out awhile, at least until you'd figured out what he really wanted. The Callahans are crazy, but they're crazy like foxes. There's a method to their madness. And I think Sam wasn't being honest with you or himself about his true motivation."

Seton shifted on her hard wooden chair in her office. "He'll have to find someone else to fill the check box on his life list."

"Maybe that's not all Sam wants."

"It's all he thinks he wants," Seton pointed out.

Sabrina laughed. "I don't remember any of the Callahan brothers going down easily."

"We have nothing in common," Seton assured her older sister, "and I don't want a second failed marriage." She idly rearranged the pencils and pens in her desk. "What would you do if Jonas came to you with the same proposition?"

"Why do you bring up Jonas?"

Seton heard the sudden tension in her sister's voice. "Sam seems to think Jonas is calling you for a reason."

"Probably. The Callahans do very little without a reason. It's usually nothing that reveals itself to a serene mind, though. And I aim for serenity, as you know. So I don't think about why he calls. I just chat with him for a minute or two until he gets it out of his system, and then I make an excuse to get off the phone."

Seton wrinkled her nose. "Still, what would you do if Jonas offered you what Sam offered me?"

There was silence for a few moments. "Well," Sabrina said, "since I'm pregnant, I'd very likely say yes."

"What?" Seton was so flustered she didn't know what to say. It was impossible to imagine her sister being pregnant. Sabrina hadn't had a boyfriend in— "Is it Jonas's?"

"Yes. But you can't tell him."

"Wait." Seton leaned back in the chair, stretching her feet out in front of her and slipping off her pumps. Her head ached, her feet ached and her whole world seemed to be spinning on a twisted axis since she'd returned to Diablo. "When you did you two have a thing?"

"A fling," Sabrina said, "and it happened when I was living upstairs at the Callahans."

Seton frowned. "You two were certainly quiet about it. No one seems to know that you and Jonas were even interested in each other."

"We're not. Just because I'm pregnant doesn't mean it was a serious relationship. In spite of my best efforts and my diaphragm, I seem to have fallen under the Callahan charm."

"Congratulations," Seton said. "What do you mean, you're not going to tell him? You're planning to, right?"

She waited with some alarm for her sister's answer. Which turned out to be exactly what she'd feared.

"No, I'm not. Jonas doesn't want children, and he doesn't want to get married. He was having a grand time watching his brothers rush to the altar, and planned on being the sole Callahan bachelor. He's already bought his own piece of property, Dark Diablo. I'm not sure anyone knows he's actually made the purchase. I can't tell you how many times Jonas told me that Fiona might run his brothers around with her Grand Plan, but he'd figured out the best way to avoid the whole thing altogether."

"I can't believe this," Seton murmured. "I'm going to be an aunt."

"Not if you give away my secret," her sister said. "I'll revoke aunt privileges."

Seton frowned. "I think your pregnancy will be obvious when you come back to Diablo, Sabrina."

"I don't plan on coming back. Ever."

"You have to tell him sometime." Seton felt as if the tables had been turned between the older sister and the younger, and now she was in charge of the scolding. "It's not fair to the baby not to know his father."

"That comes later," Sabrina said. "Trust me, I have a plan. After the baby is born, I'll tell him."

Seton frowned again. "Why after?"

"Because all the Callahans have managed to get married *before* their babies were born, as I recall, or very shortly thereafter. I don't want Jonas suffering a similar attack of conscience."

"That's terrible," Seton said. "What about the poor child?"

"The poor child will be fine. I'm sure that he or she will later appreciate that I didn't try to tie Dad down."

"I don't know," Seton murmured slowly, and Sabrina said, "Back to your question."

"What question?"

"About Sam's proposal."

"Actually, the question that got us here was what would you say if Jonas offered you the same proposal. You said you'd accept!" Seton exclaimed with delight. "Therefore, it only makes sense for you to tell him."

"The proposal under consideration," Sabrina reminded her, "is 'marry me, Seton, and it'll be a name-only thing, just to satisfy the family requirements.' I would take that deal. But I'm not being offered anything by Jonas."

"But you might be!" Seton felt compelled to fight for her niece or nephew's sake. After all, aunts were meant to be advocates, weren't they? "If you'd tell him!"

"The difference is, your deal is that there'll be no babies, no sex," Sabrina pointed out. "I can assure you that Jonas and I could never strike that bargain. Obviously, we've already had sex, and if we got within a mile of each other, we probably would again. But you and Sam—"

"Never would," Seton said, somewhat morosely. "He made that pretty clear."

"Exactly. So you're in a stronger position."

"Why?" Seton flexed her feet and shoved them back into her pumps. Her head was spinning, and she was ready to head out into the already dark street of Diablo. "You're having a baby. I want a baby, and won't get one from Sam."

"I'll leave you to figure out those details," Sabrina said.

Seton flipped off her office lights and locked the door, stuffing her keys into her briefcase as she walked down the hall, cell phone to her ear. "Don't you want to wear the magic wedding gown? It's yours, Sabrina, after all."

"No, I don't. It was Mom's, Seton. It's only magic because it was Mom's. I had nothing to do with that. I've been thrilled for other women to wear it and know their true love. Me? I'm just happy I'm going to be a mother, to be honest."

Seton headed out into the brisk night air and glanced up at the stars. "I miss you. I can't bear that you won't ever come back to Diablo. Why didn't you tell me that when I was in D.C. with you?"

"Because I had a strong feeling there was someplace else you belonged. And I've really gotten into this animal activist stuff," Sabrina said. "That undercover investigation we did with the circus really fired me up. There's a whole lot I can do, Seton. Next week, I get to speak before a committee on animal abuse. I like it here in D.C. And it'll be a great place to raise a child."

"Sure," Seton said, not convinced. "Thanks for the chat, sis."

"No problem. Go get him, is my advice."

"I don't want—" Seton began, but Sabrina had already hung up. "I don't want him," she murmured, walking to her car, not noticing the figure leaning against the door.

"Working late?" Sam asked, and Seton gasped.

"Sam!" She tossed her cell into her briefcase, feeling a little guilty about talking about him. She hoped he hadn't heard anything she'd said. "What are you doing?"

"Waiting on you. How about we discuss things over a drink at Banger's?"

Seton looked at Sam, thinking about her sister's pregnancy. She couldn't have a drink with Sam. If she did, she might start talking and unload Sabrina's secret. It weighed so heavily on her now. "I don't think so."

"C'mon," Sam said, "you look like you could use a chardonnay."

"I could," Seton said, "but I think Aunt Corinne is waiting on me with tea and cookies."

"Nah. She's playing bingo. I just saw her at the Books'n'Bingo with the blue-haired crowd. That means," Sam said, with his trademark Callahan smile, "that I'm all yours for the evening, doll."

Chapter Three

"I owe you an apology for my behavior earlier," Sam said. Seton rattled him more easily than anyone he could remember, and that included judges and fellow lawyers.

"No need to apologize. I shouldn't have looked for your family records."

"You were trying to help. I appreciate that. Like you said, anyone could have found the same information," Sam stated, ignoring her reluctance to accompany him by placing a hand under her elbow and guiding her toward Banger's. "However, I need a wife more than a P.I. now."

Seton pulled her arm away from his grasp and gave him a stern look. "I absolutely refuse to discuss weddings, marriage or proposals of any kind."

"Suit yourself, doll," Sam said as he led her into Banger's. "Let me take that suitcase from you. It looks so heavy for such a delicate lady."

She snatched her briefcase away. "Don't patronize me, you ape. Or you'll be sipping chardonnay with someone else tonight."

He grinned. "I like a woman with spirit. I'm sure that's obvious."

"Well, I don't like you," she returned as she slid into a booth. "So don't push your luck."

Sam grinned and told himself that if he took things real slow with Seton, maybe, just maybe, he'd end up with her in his bed eventually. Of course, that would throw off the marriage-in-name-only angle. He studied her more carefully, and wondered if marriage-in-bed-only was more his game, anyway.

SETON FELT AS IF a wolf was watching her all night long. Okay, maybe she and Sam had been at Banger's for only two hours, but she felt as if he was waiting to pounce on her. He watched her every move. She drank her wine faster, and didn't decline when he ordered taquitos and Southwestern wraps. And more wine.

Somewhere along the way, she found herself having fun. "I've had enough," Seton finally said, waving away the waiter with the liberal hand at pouring. "No more for me or I'm going to sprout grapevines."

"The night's still young."

Young enough to get in trouble. "I'd better be going, Sam." But she didn't move. It was cozy in Banger's, and the booth they'd been given was private and lit by candles. Seton told herself to relax; Sam wasn't going to spring on her. And the fact that her sister was pregnant by his brother shouldn't make her uneasy.

Of course, it did. She was worried for Sabrina, and Jonas, and the baby. The situation gnawed at her. Seton sipped at her wine, reminding herself that her sister's life was her own.

"Jonas is driving me nuts," Sam said. "He spends all his time hanging around the ranch. He won't go out.

He's about as much fun as wet socks. I don't know what his problem is."

Seton shook her head. "Ask him."

"He grunts by way of pleasantries these days." Sam gazed at her. "How's Sabrina, anyway?"

"Enjoying what she's doing, I think." Seton stared at Sam's mouth and fleetingly wished they were kissing and not talking as if they were just friends.

He drummed his fingers on the table. "I don't suppose she'll be coming back to Diablo anytime soon."

"I don't think so."

"That's too bad. A little female companionship might be good for Jonas."

Sam seemed genuinely worried about his brother. Seton had nothing to say that would relieve either of them, so she shrugged. "Thank you for a lovely meal, but I—"

He put a hand over hers as she clutched her purse. "Don't go just yet."

"Sam." The temptation was too strong. His warm fingers on hers sent waves of longing through her. She didn't want to acknowledge any feelings she might have for him at this point. Those feelings she'd had before—the questions that had brought her back to Diablo—simply couldn't exist any longer. Even if everything else could be waved away with a magic wand—such as his reluctance to have children and her strong wish for a baby—Seton couldn't date Sam in good conscience, knowing that Sabrina was pregnant with Jonas's child. "I really have to go."

She stood, surprised when Sam pressed her hand to his lips.

"Thank you for spending this evening with me," he

said, his tone agreeable and a little wistful. "I really didn't want to go back to the ranch to look at Jonas's sour puss another night." Sam laid money on the table and put his hand against the curve of her back to guide her from the restaurant.

As they walked out, he waved to people he knew, and Seton was uncomfortably aware of the interested glances following them, especially from women. She wished Sam didn't have his palm against her back; it felt so possessive. Yet wasn't this why she'd returned to Diablo? To see if there could be anything between them?

"I'll walk you to your car."

Sam and Seton headed that way, crisp March breezes making them hurry faster than she would have liked. The thought made her feel a little guilty. She liked spending time with Sam, more than she should.

Sam waited while she unlocked her car. "Good night," he said. "Thanks again for having dinner with me."

Seton hesitated. "Sam, I really am sorry about digging into your family history."

He looked at her. "I think you were meant to do it," he said. "Why else would I decide I needed Nancy Drew in my life?"

Seton gazed back at him. "You mean all that proposal stuff was a ruse to get me checking into your family past?"

"No," Sam said, "the offer's still on the table. What I meant was that there are a ton of other single ladies around. I had to pick the one with a nose for solving mysteries. Maybe it was my subconscious directing me."

Seton let herself sink into the driver's seat. "Glad you weren't attracted to me or anything."

"Yeah," Sam said, "physical attraction usually has a short shelf life."

"What would you have done if I'd said yes?" she asked, curious in spite of herself. "Given that you're not attracted to me for anything except my curiosity."

"Well," Sam said, "first, I would have married you."

She wrinkled her nose. "And then?"

"We would have stayed married until you got sick of ranch life, or decided that the long hours working as a lawyer got on your nerves." He shrugged. "But you didn't say yes, so you're off the hook, lady."

"Good thing, that," Seton said, thinking about Sabrina.

"I guess that means you don't plan to change your mind."

She thought he actually looked hopeful that she might. "No," Seton said softly. "I won't."

He grinned at her. "Too bad. I would probably have shown you a good time."

She raised an eyebrow. "After we were married? Why not before? You have such a strange way of going about things."

"That's what makes me a successful lawyer," Sam said cheerfully. "I never do what the opposition expects."

"Nice to know. Good night, Sam." Seton closed the car door and pulled out of the parking lot, somewhat disappointed that he hadn't tried to kiss her good-night. He hadn't even looked as if he wanted to.

Maybe he really wasn't attracted to her. Could his proposal about a marriage-in-name-only have been sincere?

"It doesn't matter," she muttered to herself. The Cal-

lahans were already adding another baby to the clan—
they just didn't know it.

Even if she'd wanted to accept Sam's proposal, she
couldn't have done it while keeping Sabrina's secret.

A small part of Seton regretted that she and Sam
could never be anything at all to each other. That secret
would always be between them.

"HOW'S THE MARRIAGE proposal going?" Jonas asked
when Sam made it back to the ranch. Since it was just
the two of them, they'd taken to living in the main house
now, giving up the bunkhouse almost for good. Sam
missed the days when Fiona and Burke had been living
upstairs, taking care of the massive, seven-chimneyed
house. He missed them in general. Now he just had
Jonas to look at.

"Slowly," Sam said, "but not as slowly as your proposal is going."

His brother waved a hand expansively as he sat in
front of the fireplace, where he was reading the *New
York Times*. "I'm not getting married. I tried it, remember? Got to the altar and everything went south. I'm not
doing that again. It's not as easy as it looks, bro."

Sam thought his older brother was being a wienie.
Despite the years between them, he felt he was the
mature one, and Jonas the lagging runt. "You and
Nancy were a hundred years ago. She's been married
with kids for the last ten, and you haven't mentioned
that old flame in five. Are you planning to sit here for
the rest of your life reading newspapers on your iPad?"

Jonas nodded, his expression serene. "Yep."

Sam sighed. "I'm going to bed. I have to be in court
tomorrow."

Jonas glanced up, removing his gaze from his stupid screen long enough to regard Sam with something like interest. "Anything about the ranch?"

"Bode's lawyers want another continuance. At the rate they're going, surely Bode'll be in his grave before this lawsuit is over. Either that or I will."

"You know," Jonas said, his tone reflective, "I would have thought once Rafe caught Bode's daughter and dragged her to the altar, the old coot would have seen that his granddaughters are going to get part of this joint, anyway."

"Yeah," Sam said. "He's pretty much disowned Julie, though."

"He's a fool." Jonas shrugged and went back to his virtual newspaper.

Sam started to say that Bode wasn't the only fool in Diablo, then decided he didn't care if Jonas turned into a pile of salt. If his brother wanted to sit in front of that fireplace like a doddering old man, that was his problem, not Sam's.

"Not me," he muttered. "There's got to be something more than a court case and Jonas in my world."

"Did you say something?" his brother yelled after him.

"No!" Sam went on up the stairs and wondered if he could talk Seton into having dinner with him again tomorrow night.

Anything to keep him from ending up like the Odd Couple with his brother.

"DINNER TONIGHT?" Sam asked, poking his head into Seton's office at five o'clock Monday afternoon.

She closed up her briefcase and shook her head. "It's probably not a good idea, Sam."

"I'm in the mood for Chinese," he said. "Surely you can't resist that?"

She looked at him, tempted in spite of herself. "I really must resist." *You and the Chinese food.*

"*Can't* is such a funny word," Sam said. "It means you want to, but are making the conscious decision to decline your better judgment. You pick the restaurant. I'm easy." He flung himself into one of the leather chairs facing her desk and shook his head. "Please say yes. It saves me from having to look at Jonas. I've had a long day in court, and trust me, I'd rather look at you than him."

Seton shook her head. "Poor Jonas."

"Poor Jonas nothing. He's calcifying in front of the fireplace. It's not a pretty sight."

Seton wondered if it was possible—even remotely—that Jonas was hankering for Sabrina. "That doesn't sound like the Jonas I remember."

"Yeah, he's a butthead." Sam glanced around her office. "You need some pictures on the walls."

"Decorating isn't my strong suit." Seton walked to her office door.

"Good to know. I nearly married you."

She laughed. "No, you didn't. I never came close to accepting your proposal. So forget about it."

"All right." Sam stood and joined her in the doorway. "Maybe we should try to fix Jonas and Sabrina up. Get them together somehow."

Seton stared up at Sam. "I don't think so. I did all the meddling I'm going to do when I dug around for information on you. I've given up on it."

"You're a P.I. Being nosy is your game."

"But meddling isn't." She snapped off the lights and locked the door.

"He's never going after her," Sam said, and Seton glanced up at him, her heart suddenly lurching.

"No?"

Sam shook his head. "Nope. He's too, I don't know, mature or something. At least he thinks he is."

"Oh." She was conscious that Sam had taken her elbow while she wondered about Sabrina and Jonas. What if Jonas did go see her sister? What if—

She'd promised Sabrina to keep her secret. "My sister certainly won't come back to Diablo."

They walked into the local Chinese restaurant and Seton felt herself relaxing in the soothing atmosphere.

"What did Jonas do to her? I'll pound him, I promise. He's had it coming to him for a while."

Seton started, not relaxed anymore. "Why would you think he'd done something to Sabrina?"

"If she won't come back here, and he won't go there, although he calls her often, then he's done something. Trust me, I know Jonas. He's a great heart surgeon, but that's all he knows about matters concerning the heart. Want to go all-out on a pupu platter?"

"That actually sounds delicious." Seton's mind was spinning about Jonas and Sabrina. She eyed Sam as he studied the menu, thinking that it was a shame the two of them had such opposite life goals.

"I suppose we wouldn't have to get married to satisfy my needs," Sam said, and Seton said, "What needs?"

"Marital needs," he said, not looking up from the menu. "My desire to have a wife, stability and peace and quiet."

"You may be the only man who equates marriage with peace and quiet," Seton observed, and sipped her sake.

"What if we got engaged," Sam said thoughtfully, his gaze no longer on the menu but on her, which set her heart pounding as she realized he was working on a Callahan plot. "Just engaged, a really long-term engagement?"

"Your point?" she asked.

"I'd be as good as married, and you wouldn't be afraid of getting tied down. Best of all, Sabrina would probably come home to our engagement party."

Seton stared at him. "That's the dumbest thing I ever heard."

Sam blinked. "Which part?"

"All of it. Order the pupu platter. I can't plot on an empty stomach."

He asked for a pupu platter and veggie egg rolls and maybe some dim sum—she wasn't paying attention to anything but Sam's face as he ordered—and then looked at her earnestly. "This could work."

"I'm not following," she said cautiously.

"They just need to be brought together," Sam explained. "Then they could both move on with their lives, for better or worse."

Seton had forgotten to ask how far along her sister was. She'd been too shocked to do so. She counted back how long it had been since Sabrina and she had left for D.C. It had been around four months.

Sabrina should definitely be showing.

"I don't think she'd come back even to an engagement party," Seton said. "Not that I'm considering a fake engagement to you, anyway."

"You should," Sam said. "There would be many pluses to being my fiancée."

"I can't think of a single one." She dragged a crispy noodle through some sauce and munched it happily. "Besides, if Sabrina wouldn't come back to Diablo, we'd be engaged for nothing. Then we'd have to break it, which would be a mess, and—"

"What if I told you," Sam said slowly, thoughtfully, quietly, in a tone she'd never heard from him before, "that I wasn't entirely opposed to having a baby?"

Seton blinked, nearly choking on her sake, which made her eyes water. She coughed and shook her head. "You're so manipulative it's scary. Or impressive. I can't decide."

"I'm serious," Sam said. "I could tell as soon as I proposed that a baby was going to be your sticking point. As you said, both parties have to get something in an agreement. I'd get a wife and you'd get a baby. Stick that coin in your baby meter and see if it registers."

She gave him a stern look and dabbed at her eyes with the white dinner napkin. "Sam, parenthood shouldn't be negotiated. Babies aren't bargaining chips."

"No, they're more like time bombs. Trust me, there's several of them ticking away around the ranch, and something's always going off." He looked pretty cheerful about his observation. "One more would just add to the energy."

He was already having one more Callahan. Seton shook her head. Their pupu platter arrived, along with more goodies Sam had ordered, and Seton dug in, hoping he would eat, too, and forget all about his newest idea. "This is delicious."

"I know. This restaurant is great. They'll deliver out

to the ranch, too, which makes all of us very happy."
Sam frowned. "Jonas has quit cooking, and it's really a
pain."

"Can't you warm up a burger for yourself? Open a
bag of Bertolli?" Seton looked at him curiously as she
bit into an egg roll and moaned with joy. "I've never had
egg rolls as good as they serve here. I literally craved
them when I was in D.C."

"Another reason you should never have left." Sam
waved his at her before dipping it in mustard and plum
sauces. "When your aunt told me you were returning,
I knew you belonged in Diablo. 'That's my girl,' I told
your aunt, and later, I realized that's exactly what I
meant."

Seton put down her egg roll. "What, exactly, did you
realize you meant?"

"That you were my girl. Or you should be. How many
times do I have to tell you I need a wife?" Sam gazed
at her. "Your aunt warned me that you might be a little
stubborn. I told her I could handle it." He started on the
dim sum with gusto.

"Maybe I don't want to be your girl," Seton said with
some heat. "You know, in some places, in a lot of places,
this domineering attitude of yours could be construed
as chauvinism."

"Nope. Desire." Sam closed his eyes as he licked his
fingers. "This is so good I could eat it for breakfast."

Seton sighed and joined him in eating the dim sum.
"Sam, you were quite certain you didn't want children."

"But I've had time to reconsider my position," he
said, "and you'd be cute pregnant. You're tall, but not
too tall, and have nice curves, so you'll be a stunner. Sa-

brina's short and has that bright red hair, so she'd probably look like a plump, cute—"

"Ugh," Seton said, "don't talk about it."

"Why?" Sam looked at her. "I just meant that you'd be very beautiful carrying a baby, Seton. And I'm willing to make that happen."

"How?" she asked, with some acerbity. "Didn't you say that our fakey thing would be in name only?"

"I'm flexible." Sam grinned at her, and Seton's heart jumped.

"Flexible."

"Sure. See how hard I'm trying to make this agreement work?"

"I wasn't aware we were negotiating."

"Aren't we?" Sam poured some more sake into her cup.

"I don't think so." Seton stared at him, wondering what it was he really wanted. Corinne and Sabrina had both said that there was more to Sam's offer than it seemed. Seton wondered if they were right.

"We have to get those two back together somehow," Sam said. "All parties benefit."

"I thought you weren't attracted to me."

Surprise crossed Sam's face. "Did I say that?"

"You said something like it."

Sam laughed out loud. "Give me a chance, angel face."

"This is so crazy," Seton said under her breath. "You're absolutely nutty."

"Probably," Sam said cheerfully. "But I can tell you like me, even if you don't know why."

Her lips twisted. "My, what a big ego you have, wolfie."

"Needs a good woman to keep it in check." Sam didn't seem too bothered by that. "Think of how much fun we could have trying to start a baby. Practice makes perfect, I hear."

She stared at him. "I doubt it."

"Well, we'd know in nine months," Sam said. "We probably shouldn't waste any time finding out."

Seton eased back, so full that she felt stuffed, and so annoyed with Sam she didn't know what to think.

"I understand that you need a guarantee," he continued. "I wouldn't buy a horse without checking it out thoroughly, either. We could give it a few months, see if the stork has room in his calendar for us, and then announce our engagement. Or marriage, whichever you're in the mood for at that time. Then Sabrina would come home for your baby shower—"

Seton narrowed her eyes. "You seem very determined to get my sister back to Diablo. What's with that?"

"My brother's suffering," Sam said. "You'd pity him if you saw him. He's practically wasting away."

"Not over Sabrina." Seton wondered exactly what had transpired between Sabrina and Jonas that she hadn't noticed. A pregnancy, for one thing.

But how much else? Was her sister in love?

Maybe Seton owed it to her future niece or nephew to find out.

"Think it over," Sam said. "Very little downside for you. If you were a gambling woman—"

"I'm not," she snapped. "I see the odds as being very long that any of this works out."

"Tell you what." He leaned forward, his voice soft enough for only her to hear. "If we find ourselves with a baby, I'll sign over my portion of the ranch to the child."

Seton blinked. "Why?"

"It'd be theirs in due time, anyway," Sam said, eternally optimistic, "and you'd have a better place for your office than that dingy building you're in now."

"I like my office," Seton said. "It's my own private space."

"You'd like the ranch better," Sam told her. "Office and nursery in one."

She wasn't going to succumb to the lure he presented. For Sabrina, maybe. But it was a long shot. Seton didn't know if her sister even liked Jonas.

She'd liked him well enough to make love with him.

"This is terrible," Seton groaned. "You have no idea the dilemma I'm in."

"It's hard pushing the upper end of your ovarian best-by date," Sam said sympathetically.

"I'm twenty-six, thank you very much," she retorted. "And that's not what I meant, anyway. I can't even imagine myself in bed with you, Sam."

He grinned. "That's funny, because I can see myself in bed with you—and liking it. A *lot*."

Chapter Four

"I don't know." Seton glared at him. "I doubt we're compatible. I think I'd prefer a more clinical route."

"Like artificial insemination?" Sam looked depressed. "Give a guy a chance, will you?"

"Clinical might be easier." The attraction Seton felt for Sam was overwhelming, but she wasn't about to admit it. It seemed as if the best route was to deny any and all thoughts of sex between them.

One unplanned pregnancy in the McKinley family was enough at the moment.

Sam grabbed her hand across the tabletop and pulled her around to his side, making room for her to sit next to him in the booth. "See, you're not exactly my polar opposite."

"I have a feeling I should be pushing away from you like one," Seton said. "Ask me later if I regret not running like heck."

"I had you pegged as a girl who likes to be caught."

"You'd be wrong." Seton leaned away from him when she noticed Sam checking out her lips. "I was on the cross-country team in high school."

He brightened. "We need an athletic woman in the

family. It's good for the genes. None of us were much for track."

Seton sighed. "I don't think you're ever serious about anything."

"There you'd be wrong. I'm serious about everything."

She shook her head. "Why don't you just ask Jonas what's bugging him? Maybe he's upset about something."

"He is. He's been mopey ever since your sister left. It's like looking at Droopy Dog."

"I'll just ask Sabrina if she'll come visit me and Aunt Corinne." She knew her sister wouldn't, though.

"You do that. Maybe it'll work. In the meantime, I'll go have blood drawn."

"You're serious about this."

"Very serious. Dead serious."

Seton looked down at her fingers, then at Sam. "I don't think so. It's not going to be easy for me to get pregnant, and if I did, you strike me as the kind of man who'd be determined to drag me to the altar."

"Well, as you're not certain you can conceive, we don't have to worry about a pregnancy yet." Sam smiled at her. "I say we go for a practice run."

"Sam." Seton frowned. "I'm not going to just go jump in bed with you when we haven't even kissed."

He leaned over and kissed her on the lips, in plain view of everyone at the Chinese restaurant in Diablo. "Mmm," he said, "I do love Chinese food."

She blushed. "I'm sure it's a rare man who claims to love sake kisses."

"Eat a fortune cookie and let me kiss you again," he teased. "Just for comparison."

Seton stood, looking at him while feeling everything was all wrong. "I can't do this, Sam."

"All right," he said, signing the bill. "Don't say I didn't offer you a whale of a deal."

They walked out together, and she was relieved when he didn't put his hand at her back. Her mind and heart were both racing, just from thinking about Sam. And Jonas and Sabrina. And the baby. But mostly Sam, and how good his lips had felt against hers.

She hadn't expected them to feel so sexy.

"Tell you what," he said, walking her to her car. "I'm going to be at a cute little bunkhouse on my property. If you're in the mood later to come by and iron out some details, I'll be there, reading briefs. No worries if you don't."

Seton watched as he took her hand and brushed her fingers against his lips. Her pulse quickened, making her nervously aware of how much she liked him. She'd come back to Diablo for this man.

And he was offering her almost everything she'd dreamed of.

Not love, of course. But just about everything else.

Maybe Aunt Corinne is right. Maybe playing it out is the right thing to do.

She couldn't. Getting involved with Sam would just complicate matters. "I won't be there," she told him, and he shrugged.

"You know where the bunkhouse is. No one stays there anymore. Jonas lives in the main house, and when I say lives, I use the term loosely. He's more like a fireplace vampire. He comes alive to feed horses and then settles back in his Count Dracula position with his tray table in an upright and locked position."

She looked at Sam. "Would you know if anyone ever used the word *eccentric* to describe you?"

He laughed. "I'll be seeing you, Nancy Drew."

Off he went, as if he had all the confidence in the world that she'd show up. Just because he wanted her to. A snap of his fingers, and the world fell at his feet.

Well, not me, buster.

AT NINE O'CLOCK that night, the sound of pebbles hitting her window pulled Seton from her bed, where she'd been reading a whodunit by one of her favorite authors. She pulled open her window and glanced down to see Sam grinning up at her from the ground below.

"You're going to wake Aunt Corinne, you ape!" she whispered. "You're too old to be throwing stones at a lady's window!"

"You didn't come see me," Sam said. "I thought I'd pick you up."

"You're so not funny." He was like a big puppy, she decided, completely unlike the cagey barrister one saw in court. "I'm not coming down. I'm reading a book, and it's very good."

She didn't really expect him to buy her flimsy excuse, and he didn't.

"How can I find out if I want to marry you if you stay locked up in your tower?" Sam asked.

"That's a problem you'll have to resolve on your own. Now go away." Seton started to close her window, then heard her aunt's voice on the porch.

"Hello, Corinne," Sam said. "Yes, it is a lovely night." Seton eavesdropped shamelessly.

"I'd love to come inside. Thank you, Corinne," he said. She realized he'd gone into the house with her aunt.

There was nothing she could do except get dressed and go downstairs. Somehow, she'd have to run Sam off before her aunt plied him with tea and cookies and questions about his aunt Fiona and uncle Burke. There was nothing Aunt Corinne would love more than to catch up on her dear friend.

Seton jumped into a blue dress, pulled a brush through her hair, gargled, smoothed on some lipstick and flew down the stairs. Sam had his head under the sink, looking at the pipes. Aunt Corinne held the flashlight and a box of tools at the ready.

"Aunt Corinne!" Seton exclaimed.

"Ow!" Sam started and banged his head on the cabinet, and Aunt Corinne jumped like a cat startled by a barking dog.

"Seton! I thought you were asleep!" her aunt exclaimed. "What are you doing up?"

Sam raised a quizzical brow and grinned.

"I'm...I thought I heard voices," she said. She gazed back at Sam, annoyed.

"Sam's come to fix my sink," Corinne said. "I saw him in town and told him I was having issues with it, and he said he'd stop by."

Seton glared at Sam, who shrugged. "Did he really?"

"Yes," Sam said, "and it turns out you did drop your ring down the drain, Corinne." He handed it to her and winked at Seton. "She thought she had, but didn't have her glasses on at the time."

"You didn't mention that to me," Seton said. "I could have helped you look for it. You didn't need to bother Sam, Aunt Corinne."

"Oh, Sam's never minded helping me out." Corinne's

expression was blithe. "None of the Callahan boys mind coming by because I give them lots of cookies."

Sam smiled. "I actually come to see your aunt. The cookies are merely a nice benefit."

"Oh, you rascal." Corinne handed him a wrench. "Thank you, Sam. Now you wash up and we'll all have a snack. I've baked some Toll House cookies fresh, and they're my best batch in weeks."

Seton frowned. "Surely we could send Sam home with his cookies, Aunt? I'm certain he has a busy day tomorrow, and it is late—"

"Why, Seton." Corinne handed Sam a dish towel to dry his hands. "No one goes to bed at nine o'clock."

Seton blushed. She'd been in bed with her book earlier. "Since everything seems to be handled down here," she said. "I believe I'll go back up to bed."

"You do that," Sam said, and her aunt smiled.

"Yes, Seton. Get your rest, dear."

She hadn't really wanted to go upstairs while Sam was here. Clearly, he couldn't take a hint to go. Seton pursed her lips, trying to decide what to do—had he not just asked her why she hadn't shown up at his place?—and decided to call his bluff. "All right," she said brightly. "Good night, all."

She forced herself to go back upstairs, and felt like a child who'd gotten sent to bed early. But she was doing the right thing. Sam hadn't said a word about coming by to help out her aunt. He was playing games with her and the best thing to do was ignore him.

It wasn't going to be easy when she could hear Sam and her aunt downstairs laughing and reminiscing. Seton sighed and tried to focus on the mystery, which no longer seemed that riveting. After a while, unable to concentrate, she put the book down and tried to hear what they were saying.

Twenty minutes later, she heard the front door open and Aunt Corinne call, "Good night!"

Sam said, "Good night!" Seton heard his truck pull away and realized she'd closed her book. She'd never be able to concentrate on the red herrings now.

Sam stayed on her mind too much these days.

"Seton?"

"Yes, Aunt Corinne? Come in."

"He's gone." She entered and sat on the vanity chair. "Didn't you want to see Sam?"

Seton wondered if her aunt had dropped her ring down the drain on purpose just to get Sam and her niece in the same room together. "I don't know," she said. "We've had dinner together the past few nights. He keeps mentioning his proposal like he means it. Frankly, I'm confused."

"He seems honestly interested in you."

Seton wondered if Sam was interested or just being expedient about his plans. "I don't know, Aunt Corinne. I'm not skilled in the dating game, I guess."

"Hiding up here is no way to encourage him," her aunt pointed out.

"I don't really want to encourage him," Seton said. "I think we might be too different."

"You came back because of Sam," Corinne reminded her.

"I know." She shook her head. "I don't know what he really wants."

"He wants a woman," Corinne said. "He wants you."

Seton blinked at her aunt's frankness. "He doesn't know me."

"What's to know? You like him, he likes you. There's no perfect rubric for love, Seton."

She sighed. "He wanted me to visit him tonight."

Aunt Corinne gazed at her. "What can it hurt?"

She didn't know. Nothing, except her heart, of course. But maybe she was worrying too much. Seton got up, began to put her dress back on. "I'll go. But I feel stupid."

"Why? Because he wants you to come over, and you want to go?" Corinne shook her head this time. "If you like the man, show up. You've practically got a steel cage wrapped around you, Seton." Her aunt smiled to take the sting out of her words. "Sam's a very nice, eligible bachelor. He likes you. What does it hurt to go find out if you like him?"

Seton hesitated, not certain she was doing the right thing. She was a little intimidated by Sam and his potent, blatant allure. But if her aunt thought paying a man a call at his bunkhouse was a good idea, then what *could* go wrong?

THIRTY MINUTES LATER, when she finally got up the courage to knock on the bunkhouse door, what Seton most feared came to pass.

Lacey MacIntyre opened the door, and Seton could see Wendy Collins, the town's much-married-and-on-the-hunt-again librarian in the background. "Hi, Seton. What are you doing here?" Lacey asked without much enthusiasm.

Cold wind seemed to whip through her. "I think I've made a mis—"

"Hi, Seton. You made it." Sam peered around Lacey with a big grin on his face. "I knew you would."

"I don't think you did know I'd come by," Seton said, staring doubtfully at Lacey and Wendy. Wendy was a sultry brunette who loved men, and Lacey was a petite, built blonde who adored men like kids loved candy. "Even I didn't know I would." She wished she hadn't.

"Well, you're here now. She's picking me up," Sam said conversationally to Wendy and Lacey. "It was good seeing you ladies, but I must be off."

"Must you?" Lacey asked with a glare for Seton.

"Yes," Sam said, putting his arm around Seton's waist. "But I'm sure I'll be seeing you soon."

Seton stiffened like a porcupine. She tried to dislodge Sam's arm from her waist, but he hung on, guiding her away from his friends and out to her car.

"You rascal!" Seton said. "How could you sweet-talk me and my aunt and have company waiting on you?"

He kissed her temple. "You have a jealous streak, Miss McKinley."

"I do not!" Seton pulled away and put a hand against a chest that felt very firm and warm. She resisted the urge to splay her fingers to feel more. "You're a louse with your harebrained proposal."

He grinned at her. "Let's go for a drive."

"Let's not." She was too annoyed to consider being stuck in a vehicle with him. "Have you proposed to them, too?"

"No," Sam said, "you were first on my list."

She knew he was teasing her but couldn't help her outraged response. "First!"

"It's a short list." He tugged her toward his truck. "We'll go in my ride. That way I know you won't drive me out and drop me off somewhere far from home, considering your current mood." He didn't sound too worried about it, though.

"It's a thought," Seton said. "Why did you have those women there?"

Sam pulled out of the driveway. "They weren't there to see me. They came to see Jonas."

"Jonas!" A sense of panic fluttered through Seton. "Those two man-hunters are after your brother?"

"I'm not certain if they're after him in the way you mean—"

"They most certainly are!" Seton thought about cute, curvy Lacey in her tight pink dress, and statuesque, exotically brunette Wendy alone with Jonas. "I thought you wanted us to have a fake engagement so Sabrina would come home to an engagement party, and then she and Jonas would bump into each other. Or some scatterbrained plan like that."

"Yeah, we may not have time for all that, considering the look of things," Sam said.

"The look of what things?" Seton was worried about her sister. If Jonas was entertaining experienced man magnets, Sabrina was going to end up with a fatherless child.

"Jonas is so mopey that the ladies are anxious to try to cheer him up. He could fall under some woman's spell. It happens to men who have broken hearts."

"Broken heart?" Seton frowned. "You seem convinced that Jonas liked Sabrina."

"It's just a hunch. But now that the ladies have come calling, could you blame him for finding comfort where he can?"

Sam glanced at her, but Seton didn't notice. Lost in worry, she watched the headlights passing occasionally on the country road. It didn't really matter whether Jonas was pining after Sabrina or not. What mattered was that there was an unborn child who needed its parents to find their way to each other again. Sabrina and Jonas needed to *talk,* at the minimum.

Seton had promised to keep Sabrina's secret. Yet she had the responsibility to try to make the best happen for her niece or nephew. The only way to do that was to get Sabrina back to Diablo—or get Jonas to D.C.

Seton slid her gaze to Sam. He glanced at her again at just that moment, and their eyes met, only to ricochet away.

"You seem upset," he said. "I promise you those ladies didn't come by to see me. They brought Jonas a peach pie because he loves pie so much. Wendy had some frozen peaches from last summer and she thought one of her special desserts would perk Jonas up."

"I'll just bet she did." Seton simmered at the thought. "That means Lacey has her sights on you."

"Nah," Sam said, reaching over to pat her leg. "All she brought me was a chocolate cake."

Seton whipped her head around to stare at him. "It's a wonder you don't weigh three hundred pounds with all the ladies in this town feeding you, including my aunt."

Sam smiled. "It's good to be a guy in a town with lots of appreciative females."

He was so smug and so full of himself that Seton wanted to ignore him. She couldn't do that. There was a higher issue to deal with than what she thought of Sam. "You're not really worried that your brother would fall for one of those women."

"Look. Jonas is a weird bird. He gave up his successful practice in Dallas to come here and molder like month-old bread. He stayed busy around the ranch, and I'm pretty sure he had a thing for your sister. I don't know that for a fact, but I live by my hunches and I'm usually not too far off." He glanced over to see if Seton was listening. When he realized he had her complete attention, he continued. "Not to be telling tales on my bro, but when she left, it was like all the air went out of him. Who knows what he might do next? It's Jonas. That's all I can say."

Seton closed her eyes for a moment, then looked out the passenger window. "Sam, I don't think it will work."

"What won't?"

"I don't think Sabrina would come back to Diablo for an engagement party."

"She doesn't want to see Jonas that badly?"

"I didn't say that," Seton said carefully. "I just think it would take a more serious reason to bring her back." Yet Seton knew Sabrina really had to come to Diablo.

"Could you tell her your aunt needs her?"

"I could, but she'd just wonder why I couldn't handle whatever it was. And I'm not going to lie and tell her Aunt Corinne is sick, because then she'd come home and know I'd lied."

"It's almost a straight shot to Las Vegas," Sam said cheerfully. "Just about nine hours, as the crow flies."

Seton took a deep breath. "A quickie marriage would defeat the purpose of getting Sabrina home, wouldn't it?"

"True. We'd have to get married at Rancho Diablo for it to work. And sooner rather than later, I suppose."

Seton glanced at Sam. "Are you proposing again?"

He laughed. "It would solve my situation, get your sister home to Jonas before he's snagged by an over-eager female—and in his current state, that could happen—and it would get you off the egg timer."

"I'm fine. Thanks."

What if she said yes? Could it work?

Would they later on regret getting married?

She didn't have time to find out. "I guess it might be worth a try."

Sam reached over and patted her leg again. "You're an excitable female, I can tell."

Seton shook her head. "When are we doing this?"

"Takes three days to get a marriage license, I bet. Blood work, find a priest…oh, shoot."

"What?" Seton's gaze snapped to him.

"Aunt Fiona and Uncle Burke will want to be here for the wedding."

"Were they at Rancho Diablo for Rafe's and Julie's?"

"No," Sam said, "and that's why I don't think they'll miss another one. Bode's lying low, and life is quite different from when they left. We've got to give them enough time to book flights, and that'll be just enough time for you to get cold feet." Sam glanced her way. "I don't think I can risk it."

"Trust me," Seton said grimly, "I will not back out of marrying you."

"Really?" he asked. "Finally realize my offer is a winner?"

She moved his hand off her leg. "That's right, cowboy."

"Works for me," Sam said. "I don't care how I get

you there, just so long as I do. You find a dress, and I'll take care of everything else."

"Lovely," Seton said, and felt a secret shiver that the cowboy she'd always wanted was finally going to be hers.

At least for a little while.

Chapter Five

"So I'd love for you to be my maid of honor," Seton told Sabrina the next day. "Would you?"

"Oh, Seton," she replied. "I'm so happy that you're getting married. I always knew you had a thing for Sam, but—"

Seton jumped in before her sister could say no. "Who else would I want to be my maid of honor but you?"

"All right," Sabrina said. "Of course I will."

Seton smiled. "Thank you, Sabrina."

"No need for thanks. I wouldn't miss your wedding for the world. Have you told Mom and Dad?"

"I'm going to. I wanted to talk to you first. Do they know about the bab—"

"No," Sabrina said. "So your wedding will have lots of surprises."

"Mom's going to flip when she finds out you're pregnant." Seton glanced out the window of her office, seeing Sam striding across the street toward the courthouse. She caught herself staring at him, admiring his long legs and loping walk.

I hope I'm not getting in over my head with this con we're pulling.

She realized Sabrina had been speaking while she'd

been thinking about Sam. "I'm sorry, what did you say, Sabrina?"

"I just said that she'll be excited about her first grand-baby, once the shock wears off. At least I hope she will be. So what color am I wearing?"

"I haven't decided." Seton thought the style of the gown was probably more important than the color, considering Sabrina's predicament. "How far along are you?"

Sam came into her office, and Seton felt the familiar jolt of attraction. She motioned for him to sit down.

"Five months," Sabrina said.

"What?" Seton exclaimed.

"I'm five months pregnant," her sister said, "so I think something with an empire waist might be best, and perhaps as dark a color as you can manage, maybe? I'm pretty petite, so there isn't a lot of space for baby. I already look like I'm carrying a prize-winning pump-kin."

Seton stared at Sam, swallowing past the sudden tightness in her throat. Diablo was going to be all atwitter when Sabrina returned. Jonas was going to be shocked, and Aunt Corinne… "How do you feel?" she asked.

"Like a house," Sabrina said cheerfully. "But I'm very fortunate. The doctor says I escaped the Callahan curse."

"What curse?" Seton thought she better know up front about any curse she might be bringing on her-self. Sam grinned at her, and she held up a finger to let him know she'd be off the phone in one moment. He shrugged, then reached over to take the hand she was resting on her desk in his big warm one.

Why did she feel so safe and yet so electric whenever he touched her?

"The baby bingo curse." Sabrina laughed. "Didn't you notice that almost all the Callahan pregnancies have been multiples? I think Fiona put something in the water out there."

Sam was stroking Seton's palm and driving her nuts. She could hardly concentrate on local legend when he was making her think about things she shouldn't be thinking about. "So…just one?" she asked carefully, not wanting Sam to guess what they were talking about, though he seemed much more interested in her body than her conversation. He made his way up her wrist, and Seton tried not to melt into a pool of languid *yes, whatever you want, Sam.* If he wasn't so darn sexy—

"Yes, just one," Sabrina said, snapping her back, "but I don't know the sex, so don't ask. I'm going to be as surprised as everyone else on the big day."

"It's going to be so wonderful…." Seton let her voice trail off before she could say, "wonderful to have a baby in the family." "Sabrina, listen, I've got to run, but I'll pick out a wonderful gown for you."

"You'd better." She laughed again. "I don't want to look like I'm wearing a tent when I'm standing next to the most beautiful bride Diablo has ever seen."

"You won't, I promise. I love you, sis," Seton said. "Goodbye."

"Love you, too. Say hello to handsome for me."

They hung up and Seton freed her hand from Sam's. "It's lunchtime. Your routine is usually to appear when I'm closing up shop at night. What brings you by?"

Sam leaned back in the chair, a teasing expression

on his face. "How about a wedding in five days at the ranch?"

"That fast?" Married in five days! That made Seton start thinking about wedding nights and making love… She practically shivered at the thought of being in Sam's arms.

"Cold?" Sam asked, and she quickly said, "No, no. I'm fine."

He smiled. "I've got a caterer lined up, the town grapevine ready to roll as soon as we give the signal, and I made sure my tux fits." He put a jeweler's box on her desk, and Seton's gaze jumped to his.

"What is it?" she asked, knowing but not sure she wanted to know.

"What every man gets the woman he's marrying," Sam said. "Open it."

"I— Sam, we really don't need to be super-fancy," Seton protested. "It's a fake wedding. It would feel wrong to wear a ring—"

Sam raised his brows and smiled. "In Diablo, you wear a ring or lots of gossip gets started."

"I guess so. You're right." Reluctantly, she opened the box and smiled at the sparkling diamond band. "I love it," she said. "Sam, it's perfect. It's feminine and beautiful, but not flashy. Thank you."

He nodded. "Glad you like it. Slip it on."

She hesitated. "I hadn't given any thought to rings. What about yours?"

"My what?" His expression filled with innocence she was certain was a deliberate ploy.

"Your band," Seton said.

"Oh, I'm not wearing one," Sam said, and she snapped her box closed.

"I'll get you one."

"I'm a cowboy. I can't wear a ring," Sam said, and Seton knew he was trying to get her worked up.

He was succeeding admirably.

"All your brothers wear wedding bands."

"Yeah." Sam leaned even farther back in the chair, looking completely at ease, a man of the world who made the decisions everyone else lived by. "But they're pansies."

Seton's lips thinned. She wasn't certain if she should push the ring issue. It was a marriage of convenience, after all. "If you don't want to wear a ring, it makes no difference to me," she said nonchalantly. "But I thought the purpose of us getting married was so that you'd get your part of the ranch without having to marry someone your aunt fixed you up with. And if she suspects our marriage isn't real, she may forfeit your portion."

"That's true." Sam's brow creased. "'No tricks' is in the papers she had drawn up for the ranch. And I suppose not wearing a ring would encourage other ladies to wonder if I was available."

"Probably," Seton said sweetly. "If that's what you want, I'm sure Lacey and Wendy would be happy to figure out that we have a fake marriage."

He frowned. "Since you want me to wear a ring so badly, I guess I'll swing by the jeweler's and pick one up."

"You do that," Seton said. "In the spirit of the masquerade, it's probably best."

"I just want you to be happy, my dove."

She raised an eyebrow. "Sam, don't overdo it."

He laughed and pulled an identical ring box out of

his pocket, putting it next to hers. "I'm into looking one hundred percent legitimate."

She opened the box and gazed at the plain gold band. "Simple and effective. I approve." She handed it back to him, thinking he was a rat and she was going to have to keep her wits about her or he'd be deviling her all the time.

"So put yours on." He indicated the box still sitting on her desk.

"No, thanks." She handed it back to him. "I'll wait until the big day. It'll be more meaningful that way, don't you think?"

Sam's lips quirked. "If you say so, bride."

"I do say so." She could tell he was disappointed she wouldn't put the ring on, but after the charade with his ring, it served him right. "Sabrina's going to be my maid of honor."

He raised a hand for her to high-five. "We did it!"

They slapped palms briefly, and before she knew what was happening, Sam took her hand and pressed it to his lips. Her eyes went wide. He kissed her fingers, every one, and then he said, "And not a moment too soon."

She told herself to breathe. "Too soon for what?"

"For my ham-headed brother. Wendy asked Jonas to take her shopping in Santa Fe, and he actually said yes."

All the joy went out of Seton's day. "Surely he's not falling for Wendy!"

Sam shrugged. "It's too soon for that, I think, but Sabrina better get here and stake her claim if she's going to."

Seton shook her head. Five days from now, she'd be

married, at least temporarily. And Sabrina's news would be all over town.

"I hope this is what you want," Seton said to Sam, and he winked at her and departed as her office phone rang.

Suddenly, she felt a little nervous.

Surely this wedding was the right thing to do.

AT THE MAGIC WEDDING Dress shop, Seton chose a knee-length ivory suit for herself and a deep emerald suit for Sabrina. The color would be perfect for her sister's hair and skin tone, the green refreshing and springlike. The shorter style of Seton's ivory wedding suit was modern. There was no need for long and lacy. She'd been married before, and though she'd never worn the magic wedding dress, she didn't believe in magic.

Even though she knew every other bride who wore it did become big believers in the tale.

"I have to be practical," Seton told Darla and Jackie as they checked her suit for fit. "I'm too old for fairy tales."

"But the gown was your mother's." Darla, who was married to Judah Callahan, looked at her in the mirror. "This suit is lovely, it fits you like a glove, but we've all worn the gown. Trust me, Seton. You want to, too."

"I don't think so." Seton looked at herself with satisfaction. "This is a very practical choice."

"Who wants practical on their wedding day?" Jackie asked. She was married to Pete Callahan, and they seemed happier all the time.

"This is exactly what I want. And Sabrina will be here tomorrow to have hers fitted." That was going to be more of a challenge, and the secret would be out. But there was no hope for it. Seton sighed. "I have an appointment in Santa Fe. Do you mind choosing all the appropriate accessories for me? Shoes, stockings, maybe even some small bouquets?" she asked hopefully.

"No problem," Darla said, and Jackie chimed in, "We do it all the time."

"What kind of appointment do you have, Seton?" Darla asked, opening a bridal magazine and looking at the latest fashions. "How about a bouquet like this?"

"Fine." Seton barely glanced at the page. "Thanks, girls." She went into the dressing room and changed, tossing the suit into Jackie's hands as she dashed out. "You're lifesavers, both of you. I couldn't do this without you. See you tomorrow for Sabrina's fitting!"

She ran out the door.

Jackie looked at Darla. "She's in a hurry."

Darla laughed. "We would be, too, if we were getting married in two days." She hung up the suit in a plastic bag. "I wonder where Seton's going?"

"Maybe a hair appointment." Jackie looked over the off-white pumps they had in stock, her lips pursed. "Does it seem like this is sort of a fast-food wedding?"

Darla glanced up. "What do you mean?"

"I don't know," Jackie said. "Just fast. Like hold the pickles and the mayo, extra cheese, please."

"Oh. Because she's having us pick everything out." Darla shrugged. "Seton's got a lot to do."

"Yeah." Jackie looked at the plain suit with some concern. "Not very romantic, though."

"The romance probably comes later."

"I guess so." Jackie couldn't put her finger on what exactly was bothering her. But this was Diablo, and if

Seton was keeping secrets about her and Sam's wedding, they wouldn't be kept long.

THREE HOURS LATER, Seton sat in a doctor's office in Santa Fe, looking at a young go-getter of a doctor who was probably fresh out of med school and not married long. But she'd looked up his credentials, and he was supposed to be excellent for her situation.

"Considering your health history of an ectopic pregnancy and consequent loss of a fallopian tube, yes, you may experience some difficulty in conceiving," Dr. Stewart told her. "But it's by no means impossible."

She didn't have time for a leisurely route to pregnancy. If she got a chance at conceiving, she'd need to have as much in her favor as possible. "I'm a bit worried."

"I wouldn't worry," the doctor said, "but in cases like yours we have had some success with a low dose fertility drug. It may be an appropriate choice for you to consider."

Seton's heart flared with hope. "What is it?"

"Generally, what we've experienced is that the dose is low enough not to cause multiples. Of patients who suspect that their chances of pregnancy may be reduced, those who have taken the drug have had more success in conceiving than those who didn't."

Seton felt a flash of sneakiness. Sam would never know. He wanted a wife, and she wanted a family of her own. Sam was right: her biological clock was ticking like the second hand on a watch.

"I'll try it," she told Dr. Stewart, who wrote the prescription and handed it to her.

If she and Sam ever got around to making love she wanted her one little ovary set on superboost.

"Are you sure this is what you want?" Jonas asked Sam, who sat lounging in front of the television beside his brother, lazily eating a Popsicle. They resorted to packaged desserts these days. Without Fiona around, constantly baking, any nod to the sweet tooth came from a box or plastic bag.

It wasn't awful, but Sam was kind of hoping that Seton wasn't opposed to tossing an occasional blackberry pie in the oven.

He shook his head. She was a career girl, probably not much of a cook. He licked the Popsicle stick and shrugged. "I wouldn't be marrying Seton if I didn't want to do it. Anyway, I get cold feet, and she strikes me as the kind of girl who has colder feet."

"Ugh," Jonas said. "I'll get you guys some Smartwool socks for your wedding gift."

"Thanks." Sam tossed away the stick and wondered if he wanted another one. "Sabrina's going to be her maid of honor."

Jonas perked up. Then he flattened out again, slumping in his chair, as if he'd already given up the fight.

What a loser. He should be running around getting that mangy hair cut, and at least shaving. If I don't give him a kick in the pants, he'll very likely get snagged by Wendy. He's unmotivated like that.

Never mind Jonas, you log. Kid brother to the rescue!

"I told you a long time ago I was going to be efficient about getting married," Sam said. "I always said I wasn't going to be a desperate dope like the rest of our clan. I picked the girl, I proposed, and now I'm going to marry her. It's a surgical strike, Jonas, and as a surgeon, you know you need the right tools at your disposal. You just open your mouth and say, 'Want to be my baby?' and the little lady says, 'Sure thing, hot stuff,' and next thing you know, you're off the market. Settled. Very efficient."

Jonas stared at him. "You're crazy."

Sam shrugged. "I don't have time for all that chasing our brothers did. I have my reasons for what I'm doing, and I prefer easier rather than harder."

"You always did," Jonas said sourly. "Well, I'm a type A personality, thanks. I have oldest child syndrome. I can't just target a female and bag her like I'm hunting a turkey."

Sam shrugged again. "Suit yourself."

"Okay, Mr. Efficient, Mr. Surgical Strike," Jonas said, "what's going to happen when Seton gets pregnant?"

"I plan to wear a condom that works, unlike some of our brothers. In fact, I may double wrap."

Jonas rolled his eyes. "Have you told Seton this?"

"She knows I'm all about the baby-free zone. I just want the comfort of a woman in my life, something you should understand."

"You're doing this for the ranch," Jonas said, his tone accusing. "This setup has all the earmarks of a scam. Aunt Fiona will be able to smell deceit in your game."

"Nope," Sam said. "I'm real busy, Jonas. I don't have time for rinky-dink romance. So I picked a practical girl who won't expect me to spend a lot of time groveling at her feet."

"You're a piece of work." Jonas grunted. "I'm not sure why Seton said yes to you."

Sam scratched his head. He wasn't entirely certain about that himself. She hadn't seemed overly inclined to welcome his company in the beginning. And his story about the double wrap was just for Jonas's benefit. Sam and Seton had no plans whatsoever to do the ol' sheet dance. One minute he'd thought he might not ever get the girl he'd been eyeing for some time; the next thing he knew, she was saying yes to a pretty lame proposal, if he did say so himself. It wasn't efficient, as he'd claimed to Jonas; it was more like opportunistic.

Maybe she digs me.

Not so much. Seton had barely looked at him the first couple times he'd visited her office.

Guess she really wanted to be married.

She'd already done the trip down the rose-festooned path, and hadn't sounded too happy about it.

It didn't matter. In two days, Seton was going to be Mrs. Sam Callahan. And all the pieces of his life would fall into place.

Finally, he'd belong.

"Back to this surgical strike theory of yours," Jonas said, but Sam shook his head.

"On second thought, fast-and-furious isn't your style, Jonas," he said, and his brother slumped back in his chair.

Never mind, bro. We'll get you a woman.

Somehow.

It wouldn't be easy pushing Jonas's chicken, type A butt through the eye of the needle, but Sam was bringing the needle right to his brother's door.

The rest was up to Jonas.

Thankfully, Seton was easy to work with. No fancy stuff, no games. Easy-bake bride.

Just my style.

Chapter Six

The Diablo grapevine was buzzing like a hive full of bees over Sam and Seton's upcoming quickie marriage. Everyone wanted an invite to the wedding, and everyone wanted in on the Big Secret.

It stood to reason that there was something fishy about the union, Bode Jenkins had pointed out to Seton's aunt. Corinne had stuck her nose in the air and told Bode to mind his own durn business.

"And that's what I intend to tell everyone. That mischief maker's done nothing good for the Callahans ever since the day Jeremiah and Molly Callahan came to this town," Corinne declared to her niece.

"I like Mr. Jenkins, Aunt Corinne," Seton said. "He seems harmless. When Sabrina was living in Bode's house, taking care of him, he was always nice as could be to me."

"He's always nice when he wants something. If there is a big secret, Seton, don't let me hear it from Bode."

Seton wondered if she should tell Corinne about Sabrina's pregnancy. The news was her sister's to share, but Seton felt guilty for not telling their aunt.

Seton couldn't go anywhere in Diablo without someone stopping her to ask about the wedding. How did she and Sam keep their romance so quiet? Where were they going to honeymoon? Where were they planning to live?

She tried to ward off all the well-meaning questions with a smile and noncommittal conversation. She didn't have those answers herself. With the gossip running red-hot the way it was, she could only hope she wasn't getting in over her head with this short-term marriage.

"I'm going to go pick Sabrina up from the airport now," she said to Corinne, who jumped.

"Gracious! I forgot to tell you that Sam stopped in on the Books'n'Bingo Society today and told me that he was making Jonas go get Sabrina. He said you had too much to do. In fact, I think his exact words were, 'I think my little bride has a list a mile long yet to conquer,'" Corinne said with a smile. "You've been so quiet, Seton, that I hadn't realized you were caught in a flurry of last-minute preparations."

Seton resolved to bean Sam at the first opportunity. "Excuse me, Aunt Corinne, please. I need to go call my darling bridegroom and tell him that I can take care of my own errands, like picking up my sister."

"He means well, dear," Corinne called after her. "He's a Callahan, you know. Those men think they have to take care of everything."

That was fine. Sam could be as pigheaded as he wanted to be—but he had no right to spring Jonas on her sister like this! Seton felt as if plumes of smoke were sprouting from her head. Poor Sabrina! Quickly, she started to text her sister to warn her—then put her phone away.

Sabrina hadn't planned to tell Jonas about the baby. Maybe Sam had a good idea.

Still, he had a nerve. Seton pulled out her phone again and dialed his number.

"Is this my beautiful bride?" Sam asked. "My partner in crime?"

"What do you mean, sending Jonas to get my sister?" Seton said. "Why didn't you tell me?"

"The idea hit me when I was visiting with Corinne," he replied. "It was so good I had to move on it. Then I had to call Jonas and jolly him into it. You were next on my list to phone, but trust me, I was moving at lightning speed to get all the moving parts in place."

Seton wasn't entirely mollified. "You have to discuss things with me first, Sam. What if my sister doesn't want to see Jonas right away?" Secretly, Seton knew the best thing for Sabrina and Jonas was probably to spend some time alone with each other—but Sam didn't know Sabrina was pregnant.

Her and Jonas's reunion had *awkward* written all over it.

"Sorry," Sam said. "I really am, but bright ideas shouldn't lie around growing moss. Wendy was over here again last night. I'm getting worried."

Seton closed her eyes for a moment. "It's all right," she said, feeling slightly sick at heart for her sister. "You did the right thing, all things considered."

"But from now on," Sam said magnanimously, "it's you and me against the world, beautiful. I promise."

"All right," Seton said, her attention captured by the endearment. Did Sam think she was beautiful?

"By the way," he said, interrupting her Sam lapse, "we couldn't get in touch with Aunt Fiona and Uncle Burke. So they won't be here tomorrow night for the wedding."

"I'm so sorry, Sam. I know how much that mattered to you."

"It's all right," he said. "I didn't give them much time, didn't have much to spare. And when I mentioned it to my brothers, they all said they haven't been able to reach Fiona in the last month. She and Burke might be vacationing somewhere."

"Wouldn't they tell you?" Seton wondered aloud. The P.I. in her went into instant digestion of the facts. It didn't sound like Fiona to disappear without telling her nephews. She doted on the men she'd raised.

"Hard to say. We don't call Ireland as often as we'd like. It's possible they wrote us or sent us an email and one of us hasn't checked the right email account. Anyway, I plan to swing by later to see you, so be ready, doll."

"Don't you have a bachelor party or something to go to?" Seton thought she should probably stay home with Sabrina—they had a lot to talk about. She also had to get her sister's dress fitted pronto. Luckily, Corinne was handy with a needle if there were any problems.

"It's bad luck not to see the bride the night before the wedding," Sam said. "Remember, most folks would be having a rehearsal dinner. I can't go two days without seeing my bride."

Seton frowned. "You've seen me every day for the past week, Sam."

"And we have lots of catching up to do. Be ready!"

He hung up the phone, and Seton put hers away, aware that with the slickness of a lawyer and the charm of a ladies' man, Sam had erased all her ire at him taking over her plans to pick up her sister. In fact, he seemed pretty happy to be in charge of just about everything.

Seton went back to worrying about Sabrina's surprise meeting with Jonas. Her sister was certain to be angry with her, and rightfully so. She would likely automatically assume Seton was trying to push them together, at the minimum, or force Jonas into realizing he was going to be a father, at the worst. Hopefully, she and Sam were doing the right thing.

But sometimes pushing Fate was a bad idea.

WHEN SABRINA WALKED into Seton's bedroom two hours later, as she was looking over the things Jackie and Darla had chosen for her to wear with her wedding outfit, Seton automatically smiled and started to run to hug her sister.

Then she saw her stomach—and gasped.

"Oh, Sabrina," she said to her petite, five-foot-two sister, who was now pushed so out of shape that her delicate form looked as if a baby elephant had taken up residence inside her. Seton hugged her tightly.

Sabrina let out a long breath, hugging her back. They clung together for a few moments, happy to be together again.

"Obviously, even Jonas couldn't have missed that you're in the middle stages of pregnancy." Seton pulled back to look at her. "What did he say?"

"Not much." Sabrina went to sit on the bed. "In fact, that was the most silent car ride I've ever experienced."

"I am so sorry," Seton said, getting mad at Sam all over again. "Sam made the arrangements for Jonas to pick you up, and Jonas left before I realized what Sam had done. Sam doesn't know you're expecting, Sabrina, so Jonas had no preparation."

Seton winced at the sadness on her sister's face.

"That would explain why he was so quiet. Callahans don't handle surprise very well," Sabrina said.

Seton sat down next to her sister. "Did you two talk at all?"

Sabrina sighed. "Mainly about the weather. The distance from the airport to the ranch. And then when he dropped me off here, Jonas said, 'Take care of yourself,' and I realized he didn't think the baby was his."

"What?" Seton stiffened. "Whose would it be, if not his?"

Sabrina shrugged. "The thought never seemed to occur to him. So I didn't offer any information. I was so shell-shocked at seeing him, and then realizing that he thought I was involved with someone else, that I just let it all go for the moment."

This was awful. Seton and Sam had made everything worse by dragging Sabrina back to Diablo. Their plan had failed dismally. And now they were marrying each other, when there really was no reason to do so.

Seton wasn't going to be the one to back out. She wasn't going to be a bride-on-the-run. If Sam wanted to be a groom-on-the-run, he was welcome to put on his sneakers and haul out.

She sighed. "Let's get you something to drink and maybe some of Corinne's cookies, and then let's have her look at this suit I bought for you. Maybe the lightbulb will go on over Jonas's stupid head fairly quickly."

"I wouldn't count on it," Sabrina said. "This is Jonas Callahan we're talking about."

Mr. Draw-Me-a-Map-Where-Ladies-Are-Concerned.

Seton wondered what Sam's next move would be, once he realized he'd really thrown a kink into his oldest brother's life.

"I'VE HAD SOME SHOCKERS in my life," Jonas said to Sam, as the Callahan brothers gathered together for an impromptu, informal bachelor party. "Seeing Sabrina again was hard enough. But seeing that she was several months pregnant shocked me so badly I couldn't make sense of it. Then I realized she must have met someone in Washington, D.C."

The brothers sat together in the upstairs library, where they always met for family conferences. Each held a cut-crystal tumbler and pondered his own thoughts.

"What difference does it make?" Judah asked.

"Do we care if she's got a boyfriend?" Rafe wondered.

"Seton's the only one marrying into the family. It shouldn't affect us, should it?" Creed said.

"It matters," Pete stated carefully, "because I think Jonas and Sabrina were quietly singing each other bedtime lullabies since at least around the time I began romancing Jackie."

"Wow," Sam said, staring at his older brother. "You old dog. None of us had any idea."

"I did," Pete admitted reluctantly. "I just thought Jonas had better sense."

Sam took a liberal sip from his tumbler and gawked at his oldest brother. "You're going to be a *father,* Jonas? Holy hell, that means I don't have to get married!"

"What?" all his brothers cried, in one giant explosion of disbelief.

"I can't deal with his issues right now, even though I arranged this gathering for him," Jonas said. "What do you mean, I'm going to be a father? That's not my baby Sabrina's carrying."

"Who else's would it be?" Sam asked. "C'mon, Jonas, don't be a dope."

They all stared at their eldest brother, who glanced around at them.

"Did you have a relationship of a very personal nature with Sabrina?" Creed demanded.

"Well…" Jonas said, and Pete said, "Be honest. I heard you talking together in your bedroom one night talking."

"Jonas doesn't do much talking," Judah said. "If he's in a room with a woman, he's probably—"

"Yes," Jonas said, before anyone else could dissect his personality or his love life. "Sabrina and I did have a very personal relationship. But then she left for D.C., and it was over. We both agreed it was over. We never dated." He shrugged. "We were very compatible, is all I'll say, because I'm not comfortable taking about intimate details regarding a lady friend."

"You don't have any lady friends," Sam said sourly. "We didn't think you recognized gender. Frankly, we thought you identified humans based on their EKGs and blood pressure readings."

"That's nice," Jonas said. "Thank you for your opinion of me. For your information, I like women. I like them a lot. I'm just pickier than you are. I liked Sabrina a lot."

"Yeah," Sam said, feeling slightly proud that he was the architect of the plan to make his brother face his life. "So who else do you think would be the father of her child, Sherlock?"

Jonas held up a hand. "It's not mine. I know, because she would have told me. Or she would never have left here."

"Goof," Judah said, "she might have left because she didn't think you wanted a serious relationship with her."

Sam nodded. "It's true. Any man who *only* sleeps with a woman is likely to wind up with some communication errors. Like Pete did." He grinned at his brother.

"Yeah?" Jonas glared at him. "And how is your relationship with Seton going? Since you claim you no longer need to get married now that I'm supposedly going to be a dad?"

Sam swallowed some whiskey, glanced around at his brothers. "Look, there's history here." He wasn't about to admit that he and Seton had a setup going that would make Houdini proud. "Remember in the beginning, when we learned of Fiona's plot to have us compete for the ranch? Back in the good old *simple* days of whoever had the biggest family won?"

He glared at his brothers. "And you bunch of turkeys were looking for a scapegoat. Everyone decided it should be me—one, because I'm the youngest and didn't care if you made me the fall guy. And two, I was willing to turn over the ranch to you guys, anyway. So I was elected to be the patsy."

He took a deep breath. "I said I'd do it, because this was back before the lawsuit heated up big-time."

"Wait," Jonas said, holding up a hand, "let's get some facts straight. One, you were the best lawyer around."

"I was all of almost twenty-seven," Sam said. "I was wet behind the ears."

"You'd already proved yourself in two major property litigations. You could have been hired on with any firm in the country. You were offered partner at a prestigious law firm. And pardon my saying so," Jonas said, "but you'd developed quite the reputation in your field as a major butthead to deal with before you so-called retired."

Sam wrinkled his nose. "I prefer the term *tenacious*. Thank you."

"So we knew you were our man. It had nothing to do with the fact that we saved a lot of dough keeping it in the family," Jonas said.

"That's right," their other brothers chorused.

"And as far as digging you up," Jonas said. "You were just cresting twenty-seven and thinking about packing in your career. But you didn't need to retire to the ranch."

"You did," Sam said, "and you're just barely looking thirty-five in the eye."

"Anyway," Jonas said, "Sabrina and my relationship has nothing to do with why you don't need to get married."

"Well," Sam said, looking around at his brothers for sympathy, "I no longer have to be the fall guy. You'll have a child, Jonas. All of you have children. We don't need any more. And now that you've all done your parental and wedded duties, you can turn over my portion to me, just like I was going to do for you." He grinned, feeling fully justified. This would let Seton off the hook. As much as he might dig her, she most certainly did not dig him.

He knew Seton didn't want to marry him. It stung, but a man had to suck it up sometimes.

His brothers were grumbling. Judah poured everyone another liberal splash of whiskey.

"It might not be my baby," Jonas protested.

"Well, let's do some fact finding," Rafe said. "When you and Sabrina were having your intimate moments, did you ever ride bareback?"

Jonas blinked. "She was always protected."

Pete coughed. "What the hell does that mean? You let her do all the work?"

"She used a diaphragm." Jonas glared at them.

"She did?" Judah looked thoughtful. "What were you doing this whole time? Just having fun?"

"I respected her choice," Jonas said stiffly.

"So every time you had an intimate encounter," Sam said, "she was protected. There weren't any little lazy moments."

Jonas's face turned slightly red. "There may have been a time or two, in the early morning, in the very early morning, when perhaps we weren't as—"

"That's enough." Sam shook his head. "Poor Sabrina. And you didn't even trouble yourself to think her baby might have been fathered by you. I feel sorry for her. I really do."

They all sat in silence for a few minutes.

"I still think you ought to marry Seton, since you're so in love with her," Judah said.

Sam jumped, nearly sloshing his whiskey. "Uh, I don't know."

"She's beautiful and smart as hell, and frankly, you're marrying above yourself," Pete said.

"Yeah, but maybe I shouldn't," Sam said thoughtfully. "She could do better."

"True," Jonas said, eager to turn the spotlight off of him. "But she seems crazy about you."

Seton? Crazy about him? Sam glared at Jonas. "Is this my bachelor party or not? Because so far it's been pretty lame, bro."

Jonas jumped up, eager to change the topic of conversation. "All right. On to the bachelor party part of the evening."

"Well, hurry up." Sam glanced at his watch. "I'm going over to Seton's in a bit."

"That's what you think, Dopey," Jonas said. "That whiskey's been making you talk stupid."

"Yeah," Judah said. "We're not going to let you back out of locking down the best thing you're ever going to get."

Sam glared at his brothers. "It's my call, I believe."

"So, anyway," Jonas said, appointing himself head funmeister. "Off we go to find the party. Follow me."

He left the library, and all the brothers trailed behind. Clearly, they all knew what was about to happen. Sam didn't care what they had up their collective sleeves. He wanted to go over to Seton's and tell her she was off the hook. It was almost a given that she'd clap her hands and jump up and down in celebration.

With all the brothers meeting the original stipulations of their aunt's Plan, everything was fine. He didn't have to get married, because he didn't care. And he didn't want children.

Life was good.

"Come on, slowpoke! It's your party!" Jonas called up the stairwell.

"I'm coming, damn it," Sam muttered, following his brothers down the stairs, and then down the basement steps. "Holy Christmas, you're not bringing the stripper down here, are you?"

His brothers groaned.

"What an ape. When have we ever had a stripper in the house? Fiona would have slapped us one-eyed," one of them whispered, but in the dim light of the overhead fluorescent bulbs, he couldn't identify the wise guy. Sam joined the semicircle around the fresh-packed, coffin-length scar in the ground, his skin already beginning to goose-pimple.

"Why are we here?" he demanded. "We're not touching that thing. We already tried it once. We dug it partially up, found a box, decided we didn't want to know what Fiona and Burke had hidden under the house, and reburied it. Remember?" He glanced around at his brothers. "We said that it was better to let sleeping skeletons lie, or something like that."

"Yes, we did." Jonas nodded, then looked at his brothers for confirmation. "But in the spirit of putting the past behind us, and as we haven't been able to locate Fiona, we've decided it's time for this family to know exactly what's been going on all these years. No more secrets."

Sam shook his head. "Does it have to be tonight? Isn't my bachelor party supposed to be about dirty stuff?"

"You'll be plenty grubby once you play around in that dirt. Dig." Jonas handed him a shovel.

"Why me? I'm the guest of honor!" he protested.

"We're all digging. And none of us got bachelor parties, did we?" Rafe said. "Let's settle this once and for all, Barrister."

"This is foul. And unfair." Sam took a deep breath,

knowing he, too, needed to know what was in their past. There was no reason to avoid it any longer. Hell, when Seton had tried to tell him small details, he'd run like a deer.

The time had come.

"This is not my idea of a bachelor party," Sam said, and turned over a shovelful of dirt.

Chapter Seven

It didn't take long for the six men to dig up the box, and with his scalp prickling, Sam knelt down. His brothers squatted beside him to help, trying to pull off the three locks of the pinewood footlocker.

When they finally prized it open, Sam couldn't believe his eyes.

Rows and rows of silver. Bars and bars of the stuff, lying neatly on top of each other. The Callahan men tugged the box from its hole, grunting with the weight of it.

Underneath it was another box.

"That one's got the body in it for sure," Judah said, giving Sam the heebie-jeebies.

"Shut up, ass," he told his brother. "Get down there and see if it's light enough to be lifted out."

Judah leaned way over into the hole, with Pete holding on to his boots. He thumped on the lid, which made a hollow sound. Then he tried to lift one side of the box. "I don't know how Fiona and Chief Running Bear moved all this stuff around. Remember Burke babysat us every year during their meeting, so we wouldn't stumble on their secret?"

Sam glanced around, noting a curved pole packed

beside the box. "See if you can grab that," he said, and Judah managed to work the pole up the side. He handed it to Sam, who jabbed at the lid, knocking it off and revealing the contents. The box was filled with cloth sacks, about the size of lunch bags, tied with string. Sam hooked one with his pole and pulled it up. He opened the bag, which jingled in his hands. "Silver coins. All of this is exactly like what we found in Fiona's so-called secret storage cave some months ago."

"The silver mine," Jonas said. "It must be worth a ton."

"You're the investor in the family, Jonas. Make a guess," Creed said.

"Could be hundreds of thousands of dollars," he said slowly. "Which means Fiona was hiding this from Bode Jenkins all along."

"Maybe it's not ours," Sam said. "Remember, we have no claim to the mineral rights."

"Well, let's pack it up," Rafe said. "We don't know who it belongs to, but it's definitely not ours, and frankly, I'm just glad it's not a body."

"Why didn't they put it in a bank?" Pete wondered aloud.

"Because it was safe here, and accessible. If Fiona had deposited any of this in a bank in town, people would have talked. And the secret about the silver mine wouldn't have been a legend anymore, it would have been a fact."

"A safe-deposit box would have been secret," Sam said, "but she would have needed so many it would have gotten expensive. Besides, the chief couldn't have gotten to it whenever he wanted, I guess." He shrugged. "It's probably not ours. We just own Rancho Diablo land."

They put everything back just as they'd found it, then tamped the dirt back down so it looked undisturbed.

"See?" Judah said. "You did have a dirty bachelor party."

Sam rolled his eyes. "I'm going to Seton's."

"Bad idea," Jonas said. "I just got a text saying that Sabrina's having a tough time fitting into the suit Seton picked out for her. Even Corinne's magical sewing needle may not save it. They think they may have to make a late-night run to the Magic Wedding Dress shop. Jackie and Darla said they'd meet them there, since all their husbands were over here reading *Playboy* magazines and drinking Sam under the table."

Sam grunted. "I'm pretty sure I can't back out now."

"That's right, wuss," Jonas said. "Everybody back to the library. We'll order pizza and try to live up to the girls' expectations of the rambunctious life we're living."

"I didn't want a *Playboy* magazine, anyway," Sam said, following his brothers.

I'd just like Seton in the flesh. And I have a bad feeling I may not get her.

THE NEXT TIME Sam saw Seton was at the makeshift altar on Rancho Diablo. His fiancée stood underneath a painted trellis, looking beautiful and nervous as hell.

He knew exactly how she felt.

She carried a bouquet of some kind of flowers he couldn't name, and looked gorgeous, which was to be expected because she *was* gorgeous. She made his heart thunder with longing and emotions he'd never experienced. He wanted her, and Sam knew that the only reason he hadn't been a gentleman and let her off the hook was simple.

He was selfish.

After last night's shocker, he'd known what he needed to do. Somehow he couldn't make himself give her up.

"Excuse me," someone said, and it wasn't the priest speaking. Sam turned to glance at the fifty or so guests seated in white lawn chairs that had been brought over from the church, and came face-to-face with a uniformed courier.

"Young man," Father Dowd said sternly, "we're conducting a marriage ceremony."

"Sorry," the courier said. "I have a schedule I have to keep. I make my deliveries no matter what people are doing when I arrive. Trust me, sometimes I'd rather not disturb them."

Sam snatched the letter the courier held out, and Jonas, his best man, tipped him. "Go on, now," Sam told the man, before Seton could slip away. She was so pale and looked so ready to flee that he didn't dare give her a chance to do so.

"Better open it," she told him.

"It can wait." He stuffed it in the breast pocket of his tux.

"I suppose you should," Father Dowd said, "just in case someone is protesting your marriage."

Seton gasped. "Why would they?"

"Do you often receive deliveries during official occasions?" Father Dowd asked Sam.

"Not really," Sam said, not wanting anything to keep Seton from becoming his bride. He felt urgent about it, as if he was racing against an unseen enemy. "Blast," he muttered, "I'll open it. But we're all going to feel silly when it turns out Jonas didn't pay the electric bill or something mundane like that."

No one laughed—or smiled. Behind them, the guests were starting to chatter to each other. This was not the way Sam wanted to start his marriage, such as it was. He didn't want to give Seton a chance to remember that he'd told her they could get a divorce later on, after his part of Fiona's Plan had been fulfilled. With Sabrina standing next to her with a tummy the size of a small garden shed, Seton had a lot on her mind. Now he knew why Jonas had been so tense. Sam figured he'd flip out if a baby got sprung on him, too.

"All right," he said, and tore open the envelope. He scanned the contents, his gut tightening. "This can be handled later," he said, and Jonas said, "What is it?"

"It involves the ranch." Sam didn't want to go into detail. He realized his brothers' ears were stretched out, trying to hear every word, and sighed. "The lawsuit has been terminated," he said, keeping his voice low.

"What?" Seton said.

Sabrina gasped. "Completely?"

Jonas grabbed the letter. "That's exactly what this says. This is the best news we've had in five years. Hurry up and get married so we can celebrate!"

"Wait," Seton said, and Sam's heart sank.

"I knew better than to open it," he told Father Dowd. "I blame you."

"That means you don't need to marry me," Seton said, almost on cue from the devil Sam just knew was perched on his shoulder, conducting this dreadful moment and laughing his little red ass off.

"Yes, I do," Sam said stubbornly.

"No, you don't," Seton said. "It was all about the ranch, remember?"

"I knew it!" Jonas exclaimed. "I knew you were rigging this marriage. If it wasn't rigged, you'd never land a babe like Seton."

"Hey," Seton said, her tone stern. "Sam could have gotten me."

Sam perked up at Seton's loyalty. "Really?"

"Of course." She didn't seem completely certain, but he wasn't going to quibble. If she'd said he could have gotten her under normal circumstances, maybe she was telling the truth.

Probably not, now that he thought about how hard he'd had to twist her arm.

"Yeah, right," said Judah, who'd come up to read the letter. "But who cares what Sam's doing in his love life? He ran off ol' Bode, and that's all that matters."

Sam sighed. "Could you please start this shindig?" he asked the priest, feeling testy with his brothers' teasing.

Seton said he could have gotten her. He had to hold on to that thought.

"Sam," Seton said, and Sam said, "Nothing has changed."

"Everything has changed," she insisted. "You don't need me anymore."

Oh, I need you.

"Maybe a short recess," Father Dowd suggested, and Sam practically growled, "Seton, will you marry me?"

Seton looked at him, studying his face for a moment. "Do you want me to?" she asked.

"I do," Sam said.

Seton bit her lip for one second, then nodded. "I'll marry you, Sam."

"Hurry before she changes her mind," Rafe, son-in-law to the man Sam supposedly had run off, said. "If she'll have him, he's a lucky man. And I can testify that marriage is a good, good thing."

Father Dowd looked at Seton and Sam, obviously trying to decide if both of them wanted to get married under what had turned out to be unusual circumstances.

"All right," he finally said, and began the ceremony.

SAM AND SETON'S WEDDING WAS, in a word, the most awkward one Sam had ever been to. But she was his now—though he wasn't certain why she'd actually said yes at the altar, once Bode had dropped his überbomb. No one was talking about how Sam and Seton had happened so suddenly; they were all abuzz over Sabrina's obvious pregnancy, wondering who the father was, and then guessing about why Bode Jenkins would finally give up his bitter lawsuit after all these years.

Sam could barely exhale the sigh of relief stuck in his chest. He felt he had to get away, had to escape. Diablo was closing in on him. "Hey, it's honeymoon time," he told Seton.

"We weren't planning on a honeymoon." She looked at him with big eyes.

When the priest had said, "Kiss the bride," Sam had done it with gusto. The thing was, he hadn't expected Seton's lips to be so sweet and soft. It was like kissing an angel. He wanted to spend an entire year doing nothing but kissing her. "Let's take one now. I'm a free man—no more court for me, beyond some loose ends. You're my wife now, so you don't have to work."

"Easy, cowboy. I'll always work." She sent him a semi-annoyed glance. "I have a case I'm working on, but it could wait." Then she asked curiously, "What kind of honeymoon?"

"I don't know," Sam said. "Let's get in my truck and drive until we're sick of driving, then get on a plane and fly to Australia. I just have to get out of this town. I have to get away from my family. Everything."

Seton gazed at him. "Sam, what's wrong?"

"Nothing." So much was wrong he didn't know where to start. All he knew was that if he stayed here, Seton might somehow slip away. She might go back to D.C. to help her sister with her pregnancy. Anything could happen. He needed to be alone with her, big-time. "Let's just disappear."

She blinked. "For how long?"

How long would it take for him to know that she wasn't going to skip out, now that she figured he didn't need her anymore? As she'd said, a good bargain was struck between two people who each needed something. Seton didn't need anything from him. "A week," he said at last. "Let's head off for a week."

"Who's leaving?" Jonas demanded as he overheard Sam's proposition. "Besides me?"

"What?" Seton stared at her new brother-in-law. Jonas had come over to join them where they stood near the cut wedding cake. Guests were milling and chatting, still gossiping about the big news. Sabrina and Jonas stayed so far away from each other they were like continental shelves that had split apart. "You're going to leave now?"

"I've got a flight out tomorrow. I'm going to Ireland to find Aunt Fiona and Uncle Burke."

Sam swallowed. "Are you sure you want to do that?"

Jonas looked like a haunted man. "I think it's for the best."

"You two probably need to talk. Sam, I'm going to go thank the guests, and then we can drive over to my place so I can pack," Seton said, skittering away from the tension between him and his brother.

"Ten minutes," Sam said, feeling an impending sense of doom. "You and I hit the road in ten."

"Okay." Seton gave him and Jonas a last strained glance and went off.

"Jonas, dude," Sam said, "cool down, man."

"I can't. I'm going crazy. You guys think that's my baby. But I'm telling you, Sabrina will barely speak to me. It can't be my baby, and my heart's cracking in two. I can't even be glad that ol' Bode finally gave up trying to screw us."

Jonas's cheekbones stood out like knife edges under his pained eyes. "Jeez, I'm sorry, bro," Sam said. "What a kick in the pants."

"Yeah, well. Just be sure you hold on to your girl, if this dog-and-pony-show wedding wasn't just about the ranch."

Jonas departed, and Sam snagged a bite of wedding cake on his way to find his bride. His itch to get married had started about the ranch, but now Sam knew it was about so much more.

Now that Sabrina and Jonas were farther apart than ever, Sam feared Seton might not be up for any more of his bright ideas. It seemed he'd lost a little luster in her eyes, and maybe she'd lost faith in him.

He had to convince her he wasn't just the half-baked cowboy she thought he was.

He had seven days to convince her that he was the real deal.

Chapter Eight

Seton's heart was heavy as she kissed her sister good-bye. "Sabrina, I'll be gone for a week. Then I'm all yours, for whatever you need."

Sabrina smiled. "I think you'll be your husband's from now on."

Seton shook her head. "I intend to help you with this pregnancy. Is there any way I can talk you into staying in Diablo? Aunt Corinne would love to have you, you know that. You can stay in my room, even move in there for good." She thought Sam would probably want her at the ranch, though she didn't know for certain. Things were changing so fast between them she could hardly keep up. What had started out as a proposition felt as if it was turning into something else. He'd shocked her when he'd declared that he wanted to marry her, even after knowing he no longer had a reason to need a wife.

"I'm going back to D.C." Sabrina smiled at her. "Don't worry about me. This is your big day, the biggest of your life, and I want you to be happy. I'm going to be fine."

"I know." Seton felt tears spring into her eyes. "But you're my sister. I love you better than anyone on the planet. And I want you to be happy, too. You deserve it."

"We both deserve it." Sabrina hugged her. "Now go, before your husband decides you don't need to change out of that pretty suit or pack more clothes. He looks so eager he might decide to just take off with you."

"Oh." Seton glanced at Sam, who was indeed gazing their way, trying not to barge into their goodbye, but obviously ready to leave. "He's not in a hurry because of me. I think the lawsuit thing threw him. He's a free man now."

"Not really." Sabrina laughed and hugged her once more. "I'll see you soon enough."

Seton got misty all over again and hugged her back. "I'll be there for the birth of this special baby."

"Don't tell Jonas," Sabrina said. "Promise me."

"I won't." Seton sniffed. "But he's dumb for not carrying you off and marrying you. I would never have thought Jonas would run from responsibility. Ireland, my foot," she said, anger drying up her tears.

"Ireland?" her sister asked, pulling back to look at Seton. "He's going to Ireland?"

"That's what he says." Seton blinked. "I'm so sorry, Sabrina."

She shrugged. "We were destined never to be, I suppose."

Seton didn't know whether she and Sam were particularly destined. They'd just made a bargain between them that he didn't seem overly pressed to wiggle out of. "Goodbye," she told her sister. "Thank you for being my maid of honor." Sabrina was so lovely, even pregnant, that Seton couldn't imagine how Jonas could fail to fall in love with her.

"Goodbye," she replied, just as Sam ambled over.

He gave Sabrina a hug, saying, "Take care of yourself."

Seton felt slightly mollified that Sam had plotted so hard to bring Sabrina and Jonas together. He'd meant well. It just hadn't worked out.

Sam grabbed Seton's hand, and with one last glance at her sister, the two of them sneaked off to his truck. They waved goodbye to the wedding guests, who seemed in no hurry to depart.

"Everyone's having a great time," Sam said, turning down the drive. "It was a great party."

"Yes." Seton looked out the window at Diablo as Sam drove toward Aunt Corinne's house. "But as a plan, it was an epic failure."

"Yeah," Sam said. "I didn't factor in the variable of Jonas's idiocy."

Seton looked at Sam. "Idiocy? The whole plan backfired. We can't blame all this on Jonas."

"Sure we can. Our family's been doing it for years."

"My sister has a share of the blame. She didn't exactly open up her mouth and tell him about the baby. Jonas isn't a mind reader."

"True," Sam said, "but he claims that can't possibly be his baby."

"What?" Seton was outraged. "What does he think, that my sister is—"

"That's why I say we can park most of the blame at Jonas's door. You know and I know that's his baby. It has always taken Jonas a little longer than the rest of us to follow clues."

"I'll say." Seton sat back, annoyed. "This whole thing, this whole sham, didn't come close to achieving any of our goals, and now we're married." She looked at Sam. "Married, Sam. Husband and wife."

"I know." He grinned, looking less unhappy about it than she thought he would. "Crazy, huh?"

He was crazy. She'd married a man who operated by his own rules. Seton looked out the window, pulled off the white rose-covered barrette she'd worn in her hair in lieu of a veil, and wondered when her normally practical mind had deserted her.

"Santa Fe's as good a place as any," Sam said a few hours later, as they pulled into a quaint bed-and-breakfast. "Our first honeymoon stop should be in a romantic place."

"Why?" Seton asked, getting out of the truck. "We made a business agreement."

"Yeah," Sam said, "but we just got married. It seems like romance is important on a wedding day. I'm a traditional guy."

Seton looked at the bed-and-breakfast, the bougainvillea trailing down the adobe walls, the delicious smells of artistic cuisine, the tourists meandering down the quaint streets. "I heard they have donkey trail rides here. Let's ride donkeys."

Sam laughed. "I ride horses. Did you see the beautiful horses we have at Rancho Diablo?"

"I did," Seton said. "And I've heard about the Diablos, too."

"Those we don't ride," Sam said, his face growing shadowed for a moment. "I haven't seen them in a while."

Seton looked at him. "We're going to do the donkey trail for our wedding celebration."

Sam shrugged. "Donkeys it is. Just don't say I didn't warn you that donkeys aren't what you want to ride on your wedding night."

"Why not?" she demanded.

"We'll be sore and stinky and too tired to do much of anything productive," Sam said.

"Perfect," Seton said, and went inside the bed-and-breakfast to check in and change.

CLEARLY, HIS WIFE DIDN'T have romance in mind, or he wouldn't currently be sitting upon a very stubborn, unhappy donkey that seemed to have it in for him. Sam decided Seton was probably still angry with him about springing Jonas on her unsuspecting and pregnant sister, and Sam couldn't blame her.

Seton didn't seem to be having any trouble at all with her donkey. If he hadn't known better, he would have thought she was born in the saddle. Her donkey was well-behaved, almost pleasant. Seton chatted with the guide and oohed and aahed over everything on the trail, while Sam could feel certain parts of him getting stiff and sore.

The scenery was beautiful, but he was pretty sure he'd rather be in bed with Seton. Still, their marriage agreement had never been about sex, and that's when Sam realized why he was on the back of a recalcitrant animal and not in bed with his beautiful wife.

"Hey," he said, easing his donkey—named Happy, ironically—up next to Seton's. "Are you still annoyed with me about sending Jonas to the airport to get Sabrina? In my defense, I'd like to present to the court the reminder that I had no idea Sabrina was pregnant, and I was acting in what I considered the best, most romantic interests of both parties involved."

"I know." Sabrina sighed. He thought his wife was beautiful with her hair up and wearing comfy blue jean capris. "But we made everything worse. And now it's so bad I don't think it will ever be right. That's the trouble with best intentions."

"I agree. The road to hell is paved with them." Sam looked hopeful. "But our marriage may go better."

"It may," Seton said, "except that I don't understand why you married me."

"I married you because I said I would. I'm tired of shopping around," Sam said. "You have no idea how boring it is to talk to different women every night."

Seton shook her head. "A true trial."

"So why'd you marry *me?*"

"I—" Seton glanced at him. "I don't know. We were at the altar, and—I really don't know. Maybe I got all caught up in the moment. Actually," Seton said thoughtfully, "I think I was scared, seeing what had happened to Sabrina." It couldn't have been easy on her sister to feel Jonas hadn't wanted to know that she was pregnant by him. Seton had felt so sorry for Sabrina, who had to stand at the altar with Jonas and know they would never be together.

"Don't be scared, Seton. I promise not to get you pregnant," Sam said. "Unlike my brother, I don't participate in sleepy sex."

"What does that mean?" Seton tried not to notice that Sam was the most handsome man—devil—she'd ever laid eyes on. "What is 'sleepy sex'?"

"Jonas said that a few times, when they were both tired and half-asleep, I guess, and woke up in the morning—or whenever—they just didn't, I mean, well," Sam said, clearly feeling awkward, "he didn't wrap up. But I swear I'll never make that mistake with you."

"Lovely," Sabrina said, thinking that she'd married the brother who would probably make double and triple certain he didn't get her pregnant. She sighed. "So what's the real reason you married me, if you don't want children and don't need marriage for the ranch?"

"I don't know," Sam said, looking out over the painted landscape near Santa Fe. "I think I just feel I've found part of myself with you."

"What part would that be?"

He looked at her. "The part of me that believes that I'll find myself one day."

"Sam," Seton said slowly, "I would have helped you try to find out who you are. I would help you any way I could."

He shook his head. "I mean the part of me that's content. I'm comfortable when I'm around you, Seton," Sam said. "For some reason, you make me smile. And you make me horny, too, but we're not talking about that right now." He grinned, taking the serious note out of his words, but Seton looked at her husband, not fooled a bit.

"I make you happy? You don't even know me."

He shrugged. "As I said, you also make me horny. You could focus on that part of my confession, if you'd like."

Seton shook her head. "We'll see if you're still in the mood to talk about sex when you get off that donkey."

Sam laughed. She completely underestimated his growing desire to share a wedding night with his little bride.

SAM WAS FINE when he got off the donkey after their long trail ride. He was fine while he and Seton ate in a tiny, rustic restaurant that served some of the most delicious stuffed chilies and potato cakes he'd ever had. The chilled mango dessert went down wonderfully.

It was when he and Seton started to walk back to the bed-and-breakfast that Sam realized he was sore as hell. In fact, he was stiffening up like one of Jackie's and Darla's mannequins in their wedding shop.

"Why are you limping?" Seton asked.

"Just a little crick in my leg. Legs. No worries," Sam said. "I'll still be able to do my wedding night duties by you. No charley horse will stop me."

"Fat chance," Seton said, laughing. "You look like you're eighty years old. You look like one of those sailors who used to get those funky ship diseases that made their legs bow."

"Thanks for going easy on my ego," Sam said. "You're supposed to give me a brandy and maybe a massage, and pretend not to notice that I've been brought down by a donkey. Why aren't you sore?"

Seton shrugged. "Maybe because my donkey was pretty thin. Yours had a cute barrel shape to it."

"And it was stubborn as hell. I had to fight it every step of the way. It didn't want to do anything but go off the trail."

Seton giggled. "You do look like you're in pain."

"It's nothing a hot shower won't cure," Sam said bravely, hoping like hell he was right.

Two hours later, Sam realized romance was pretty much off the table. "This is bad," he said. "I'm supposed to be romancing you."

"Not really," Seton said. "That was never in our agreement."

Sam looked at her. "I don't suppose you want to get on top?"

Seton gave him a tiny smack on the shoulder. "I'll order you some brandy. And then I'm going to sleep. I've had a lot of excitement today, you know."

"Wait," Sam said. "I'm going to fall like a tree into that bed, and then you come over and—"

"No," Seton said. "Quit being pitiful while I call room service."

"If my brothers knew that I was unable to do my husbandly thing, they'd laugh me into the next county. I'd never live it down."

"Believe me, I won't tell," Seton said. "We McKinleys know how to keep secrets."

"I noticed. Don't think I didn't notice how you two girls kept Sabrina's pregnancy under your hats. But," Sam said, "you're not a McKinley anymore. You're a Callahan."

He hoped Seton wasn't going to be one of those keep-my-own-name women, but she was pretty independent. He was lucky she was wearing his ring. Hell, he was damn lucky she was in the same room with him. "I'll make this up to you, I promise."

She hung up the phone. "Brandy's on the way. Try to relax. If the brandy doesn't work, we can see if there's a doctor who'll order you a muscle relaxer."

"Jonas could do that, but I'm too embarrassed to ask," Sam groaned. "Make sure that brandy's a big one, please."

"I ordered a bottle," Seton said, her tone sweeter than he thought was healthy. A knock sounded on the door.

"And here it is." She took the bottle, signed for it and closed the door. He watched while Seton poured him a nice tumbler and a small glass for herself.

When she handed it to him, he sighed. "This will help me relax, I'm sure."

She clinked his glass.

"To being married," he said. "It should be fun."

"To being married," Seton said, "and of course I'm keeping my own name." She drank, and after a moment, he drained his glass. There was nothing else to do. His back was beginning to draw up in places, reacting to the cramps in his legs and the tightness and the long ride on Happy's fat back. Seton refilled his glass and got in bed next to him, and they both lay against their pillows and stared at the television they hadn't bothered to turn on. A slight breeze lifted the white curtains hanging in front of the window Seton had opened, and a full moon shone in the dark velvet sky outside.

"This is romantic," Sam said.

"Yes, it is," Seton softly replied.

He turned to look at her. "I married you because I think I really like you. A helluva lot."

She sipped her brandy, then turned to him. "I married you because I think I might like you. A little bit."

"Is that your version of meeting me halfway?" Sam asked, unable to help the smile that spread to his lips.

"Yes." She reached over and topped off her drink, then his. "You have an ego the size of that moon."

He shook his head. "I hope you realize that if Fat Happy hadn't crippled me, I'd be jumping your bones right now."

Seton smiled and sipped her drink. "Dream on, cowboy."

"Well, I'd be giving it my best effort." He ran a hand down her arm. "Are you going to change out of those clothes into something more comfortable?"

"I'm going to take a nice long shower as soon as you relax."

Sam grunted. "I don't know if I can relax around you. The thing is, I've always had this thing for you. Just a small, tiny thing—"

"Oh, no," Seton said. "Disclosures like that should be made *before* the wedding."

Sam reached over and lightly pinched her arm. "Don't worry about that, lamb cake. I assure you—"

"All right," Seton said. "I can take only so much of your bragging."

He grinned. "Anyway, I think I always had a thing for you. When you went away, it kind of sucked. In fact, I was surprised by how much I wished you hadn't left Diablo."

"Really?" She gazed at him, and he drew in a breath. With the moon lighting her hair and the soft look in her eyes, he thought Seton had never been more beautiful.

"Yeah. Really." He shrugged. "So when you came back, I guess I was determined not to let you slip away again. I thought up every excuse I could to date you. I couldn't really think of anything good enough to convince you. Then I realized I needed a wife."

"But you didn't."

"I didn't know that until today. When Bode's letter arrived, I was sure you'd dash off with your freedom. I was relieved when you didn't."

"I told you, Sam. I want a baby almost as much as you don't want one." Seton refilled his glass. "You may not be the brightest bulb in the box—"

"Yeah, right." He laughed.

"Or perhaps the most handsome or understanding—"

"Mmm. If you're going to take advantage of me in my weakened state, you're going to have to use flattery."

Seton laughed out loud. "Whatever."

They sat and sipped their brandy for a few more moments, then Seton looked at him. "How's the stiffness?"

"Moving to other parts of my body."

She set down her glass. "Do you want me to call someone? Jonas?"

Sam laughed and set his glass on the bedside table. "No, thanks," he said, pulling her into his arms. "Let's see if you can make it go away."

Chapter Nine

"And that's what we did all week," Seton told her aunt after she and Sam returned from their adventures. They'd decided they liked seeing the New Mexico sights, and had explored every trail, every historic church, every sight that was on their unplanned route. "We just drove and drove in no particular direction and with no itinerary. It was so much fun."

Corinne's eyes widened. She took cookies out of the oven and slid them onto a cooling rack. "I don't know if I'd want to be in a truck for a week."

Seton smiled. "I guess it doesn't sound that spectacular. But I really enjoyed getting to spend a lot of time with Sam."

They'd made love a lot, but she wasn't going to share that detail. It was crazy how well matched she and Sam were, physically. Out of bed he still had a tendency to be stubborn and opinionated at times, but she'd noticed that the longer they were away from the ranch and his job and Diablo, the more settled down he'd become. "We almost stayed gone another week," Seton confided. "But I've got this case I'm working on, so we couldn't." She looked at her aunt. "When did Sabrina go back?"

"Oh, she didn't." Corinne turned to gaze at her. "Didn't you know?"

Seton shook her head. "We didn't talk to a single soul while we were gone. We deliberately agreed we wanted one week to ourselves just to see if we could stand each other. Sam called it forced intimacy."

"Good idea." Corinne went back to removing cookies from the cookie sheet. "Jonas went to Ireland, so Sabrina was in no hurry to leave. She'll probably go when he gets back, but who knows when that will be?" A frown creased their aunt's forehead. "Actually, she's getting far enough along that it may be better for her to stay here, something I am, in fact, hoping for."

"It would be wonderful if Sabrina has the baby in Diablo." Seton went over to help frost a batch of cookies that had already cooled. "Sam needs to be around an infant so he won't be so scared of babies."

"What do you mean, scared? There are plenty of infants out at Rancho Diablo!"

"Sam doesn't want children." Seton shrugged. "He says he doesn't know who he is, and that wouldn't be fair to any children he might have."

"He's a Callahan. What more does he want to know?"

"I don't know." Seton really didn't. But it was Sam's shadow to deal with; he'd made it plain he didn't want help with it.

"How's life in the bunkhouse?" Corinne asked.

"Bunkhouse-y. The first night we were too tired to decide if we liked it or not. It may take me a week or two to know for sure."

She was pretty certain she didn't care where she slept as long as Sam was with her. After his initial issue with the donkey, Sam had proved himself to be an enthusiastic and generous lover. It was more than she'd ever dreamed she'd find in a man, and bunkhouse or no, she was staying with him.

"You look so happy," Corinne said, and Seton smiled.

She was so happy it was hard to imagine what could ever make her doubt that she'd made the right decision when she'd married Sam.

A MONTH LATER, Sam decided Jonas was the laziest brother on the planet and needed to quit vacationing and come home. "Who does he think's going to do all the work around here?" he asked Rafe.

Rafe shrugged and kept pitching hay into the feed boxes. "We are. Anyway, he's having trouble locating Fiona and Burke."

Sam's skin chilled. "What do you mean?"

"According to the neighbor who is keeping an eye on their house, they weren't there very long. Fiona and Burke asked her to look after the place, and they left. Which explains why we haven't been able to get in touch with them. Jonas has been staying in their home. He says their answering machine is unplugged."

Sam blinked. "So she doesn't know that Bode called off the lawsuit."

"Nope." Rafe moved to another stall. "I don't know if you know this, since you've been so focused on your wife, but according to Bode, the reason he gave up his claim is that Julie told him she was going to move away—with the grandbabies."

"Were you planning to leave Rancho Diablo?" Sam asked. He couldn't believe that Rafe would.

"I didn't want to, but I was going to do whatever my little wife wanted. Trust me, when your woman has triplets, you kind of do whatever it takes to make her life easier. And Julie was getting tired of the tension between her and her father, especially once we got married. I think her basic hint was *Get along or I'm gone.*"

"Whoa," Sam said. "Go, Judge Julie."

Rafe grinned. "Funny how we've all married really independent, sort of spicy women, huh?"

"I guess." Sam frowned, remembering that Seton had told him she'd married him so she, too, could have a child. He'd told her she wasn't getting one.

She was pretty independent.

"So, about this baby thing," Sam said. "Do you feel that the triplets have furthered your relationship with Julie? Or do you wish you were still single and living the life?"

"What the hell kind of question is that?" Rafe demanded. "For such a smart man, you're definitely dumb when it comes to women. Are you trying to sell your wife that lame excuse for the DINK couple?"

Sam's temper rose. "What is a DINK, dork?"

"Dual income, no kids." Rafe glared at him. "Did Seton know up front you had no plans to become a father?"

"Yes," Sam said defensively.

"Well, then she should have left you in the pond. There's nothing greater than being a dad."

"Not everyone is cut out for it," Sam said stiffly. "I don't think I'd be a good one."

Rafe sighed. "Suit yourself. See if you like being divorced any better."

Rafe had a point. Seton hadn't said anything more about having children, but he couldn't hope that their awesome sex life would be enough to keep her satisfied. He saw her holding his brothers' children on the ranch all the time. He knew she'd be a great mother. "I'm going to go," Sam said.

Rafe glanced up. "C'mon, Sam, I didn't mean to hurt your feelings."

Sam waved at his brother and left the barn.

It was time to figure some things out.

SETON SQUEALED when the bunkhouse door opened with a crash. "Sam! Did the wind catch the door?"

He peered into the kitchen. "What are you doing up there? It looks dangerous."

She looked down at her husband from the countertop where she was dusting off kitchen shelves and storing away china and dishes they'd gotten as wedding gifts. "It's not dangerous when you don't scare me half to death by trying to take the door off its hinges."

"Sorry." Sam glared at her. "I don't think you should be doing that if I'm not here, in case you fall."

"I'm fine. Did you want something?" Seton could tell her husband had something on his mind. Whether he shared it or not remained to be seen.

"You," he said.

"Oh," Seton said. "Well, actually, Sam, I need to talk to you." It was now or never, she realized. They'd been going along for a month and a half, trying on their new marriage, getting to know each other. Things seemed fine, although sometimes she wondered what would hold them together. She and Sabrina had talked a lot, and Seton knew that a baby wasn't always the glue a marriage needed.

"Talk fast," Sam said. "The afternoon is young and I could be easily convinced to have plans for you."

Seton put away the piece of china she was holding, and sat down on the kitchen counter. Sam came over and tugged her close to him, so that their bodies met and melded.

"This isn't something I can tell you quickly." He was nibbling on her ear, but Seton was suddenly too nervous to warm up to her husband.

"Thumbnail sketch is fine," Sam said. "We have things to do."

"I'm pregnant," Seton said, and Sam pulled back to stare into her eyes. Her heart pounded, and she realized she was sinking her fingers into his forearms, trying to keep him from running away. Once she noticed her subconscious reaction, she took her hands off his arms and waited.

He swallowed hard. "Pregnant?"

She nodded.

He took a deep breath. "How? We've been so careful."

Seton drew in a breath of her own. Now was not the time to make her confession to Sam. He was already in shock. "As you probably remember, we had a very good time on our trip. There was the time in the shower, and the quickie in the back of the truck looking at the stars from the canyon—"

Sam shook his head. "It was a rhetorical question. I was pretty much talking to myself. I know how babies happen, Seton."

She swallowed at the detached tone of his voice.

"That's great. Really great. I'm going to go right now," he said, backing up. "I have some things I need to do in town."

"All right." Seton looked at her husband, knowing

he was experiencing some emotion she couldn't really understand.

"I'll see you later." Sam turned and left.

Seton went back to unpacking wedding gifts, trying not to give in to the hurt. The truth was, she'd never expected to get pregnant so easily. She hadn't during her first marriage, after she'd had the ectopic pregnancy. That relationship had gradually fallen apart when she couldn't conceive again.

She certainly hadn't expected the drugs to work so quickly. She was thrilled to be pregnant—but she knew Sam was not.

The knowledge scared her. Everything had been going along so well.

Maybe Sam was just in shock, Seton told herself. *I was, too, when I found out.*

His navy eyes had turned so flat, so strange.

Maybe he'd come back soon.

SAM TOLD HIMSELF he was being a royal jerk. He knew he was. But it was like everything in him was screaming to *run!*

He wasn't about to talk to any of his brothers about Seton's big news. His big news, too. They couldn't understand, because they weren't him. They'd never grown up knowing that they were somehow different from the rest of the family, a piece that didn't quite fit. And he couldn't really hide from that knowledge anymore, not now that he was going to be a father.

It was time to face the facts that he'd always known might come out during the lawsuit. He'd been aware that a real chance existed that whatever truth was hidden about him could have been revealed.

He'd ignored the fear and concentrated on keeping the family home. If Bode had known anything, he hadn't made a peep.

But now Sam had a reason of his own to find out what he could. It was time to finally figure out why he had, as Jonas had put it all those years ago, come later.

What Seton didn't understand was that babies were a miracle—but everyone, even children, needed to know their place in the world. And he never had.

Chapter Ten

After a month of Sam's relative silence, during which Seton was positive he was suffering over finding out he was going to be a father, he walked out of their bedroom wearing black boxer briefs that were practically painted on him. Seton blinked, and realized she hadn't seen Sam entirely nude since she'd told him about the baby.

"I've been thinking about this," Sam said, "thinking about it a lot, actually, and I've decided you can look. In fact, I'd really appreciate it if you did."

Seton's eyes widened as she put down the file she'd brought home to work on. *I certainly am looking,* she thought. "Look?"

His jaw clenched. "Do what you were doing in the beginning. When I told you to quit digging around in my past."

"Oh." Seton sank into a chair. "I can do that if you'd like."

"If you're not too busy," Sam said. "I know you've been bothered a lot by morning sickness—"

"Not that bothered," Seton said.

"Morning, noon and night. Didn't you go to the doctor because you felt so weak?"

Seton frowned, not wanting to be reminded of how

embarrassing it was to have been so sick around Sam. He'd been patient—but he also hadn't tried to make love to her. She couldn't tell if he was trying to be considerate or was displeased about the baby. Either way, she missed him holding her. "I'm fine now. I've been working for the past couple of weeks."

"Something I'm not certain you should be doing." Sam glanced at her stomach. "Shouldn't you be taking care of little Sam?"

Seton shook her head and went back to the makeshift office they'd set up in a back bedroom. "Little Samantha is just fine."

He popped his head into the room. "Do we know it's a girl?"

Seton laughed. "It's much too soon, Sam. Anyway, what specifically do you want me to look for?" She was so distracted by her half-nude husband that concentrating was difficult.

He flung himself into her office chair. "I think the best place to start is what happened to our parents. It's something we should know, and now that it's clear Fiona wasn't entirely honest with us, we'd all like to find out."

"We?" Seton took in Sam's wide, bare chest and his strong, muscled arms and shivered.

"I discussed it with my brothers. We're officially hiring you."

"You don't have to hire me." Seton didn't complain when Sam pulled her into his lap. "It shouldn't be that hard for me to find out where they're buried, at least. Someone has to have a death certificate."

Sam busied himself by peering inside her blouse. "I may like having a baby, Seton. I think you're filling out."

She playfully smacked his hand away. "Focus, Sam. This is important."

"It most certainly is." He picked her up and carried her down the hall into their bedroom. "We'll talk about it some more in about an hour."

Okay, Seton thought, as Sam held her and touched her in all the ways she liked to be touched. *An hour sounds marvelous, now that you've noticed me again.*

She'd wondered if he'd lost interest in her because of the baby. They hadn't talked about it....

"Sam," Seton said slowly, as her husband laid her on the big bed they shared, "was it because of the morning sickness that you've stayed away from me?"

He raised his head from where he'd been kissing her neck. "You seemed like you had enough to deal with." He sneaked her top down, found her bra straps of sudden interest. "This is pretty, babe. Have you been buying new lingerie?"

She smiled. "Certain changes are necessitating new purchases."

He pushed the straps off her shoulders and kissed along her collarbone. "Anyway, just for the record, I wasn't staying away from you per se. I was waiting my turn. Baby seemed to have taken over your body, and I was willing to wait. Do I get extra points for patience?"

She closed her eyes, telling herself that now was not the time to make her confession. But it had been agony when Sam had been "waiting his turn." She hadn't known why he didn't seem to desire her, yet she hadn't wanted to ask. Had feared it was because of the surprise pregnancy.

It seemed to Seton that the best thing to do would be to make a fresh start in their marriage and go forward without any more doubts, especially now that Sam seemed to trust her enough for her to look into what she knew was a very private and painful matter for him.

"Sam," she said suddenly, "I missed you."

"Not half as much as I missed you." He'd found a nipple and was torturing her, and it was all Seton could do to gently take hold of her husband's face, stopping the moment.

"I have to tell you something," she said, looking into his denim-dark eyes, "and this is not going to be easy for me."

He pulled back for a moment, staring at her intently. Seton thought she'd never seen a more sexy male. Shivers ran all over her, mixed with nervousness from her worried conscience.

"I'm listening," he said.

Seton drew a deep breath. "I was taking fertility drugs."

He blinked, pulled back from her. "What?"

She nodded, holding his gaze.

"Why? I mean, I guess the answer's obvious, but—"

"I didn't think I could get pregnant. At least not easily. And I didn't know why you were marrying me. At the time, it seemed like maybe you just wanted me in order to get the ranch. I wanted a baby more than anything." She looked down at her hands. "I guess that sounds selfish. I mean, I didn't even know if we'd ever make love. You didn't seem that interested in me that way. And I was perfectly happy when we used condoms." She looked back at Sam. "I just wanted the chance to get pregnant if we ever got around to deciding that we wanted a baby. It seemed like a very far-off eventuality, considering the parameters under which we were marrying."

Sam didn't say anything. Seton's heart seemed to contract as she felt him withdrawing from her emotionally.

After a long moment, he sighed. "I wish you'd told me in the beginning, but it's too late to worry about now. I've seen my brothers around their kids, and surely I can handle fatherhood, too."

"I know you can. We'll do it together," Seton said. "Sam, I promise I'll never keep anything else from you."

He rolled her over and gave her a tiny smack on the fanny. "You bet you won't, because I'm going to be keeping a close eye on you from now on. In fact, I noticed that you have a sonogram marked on the calendar for tomorrow, and I will be attending. Just so you know."

He got up from the bed. Seton gazed after him wistfully, realizing her husband's desire for her had dissolved. Or the mood had changed.

She was still glad she'd told him. They couldn't have a relationship with secrets between them.

"Thanks, Sam." Seton got up from the bed, too, and padded into the kitchen. "It's my eight-week sonogram, so I was hoping you'd want to see our baby."

"Well, I do." He came over and kissed her temple, then went to the door. "I'm going to finish helping my brothers with some chores. Do you mind if I tell them you'll start doing your P.I. thing on the family tree?"

Seton smiled, glad Sam was putting his trust in her. "Yes. I'll do my best."

He nodded and left.

Seton was completely aware that, although Sam

hadn't said it, she'd shaken him with her confession. She'd felt a split form in their relationship, though he'd tried to sound as if everything was all right.

She knew it wasn't.

DR. GRAYBILL SMILED WIDELY as he looked at Sam and Seton the next afternoon. "Quadruplets," he said. "Don't see those very often. Congratulations, Mom and Dad."

"What?" Sam's question was like a thunderclap in the small room. The nurse and technician chuckled at his shock. "Four babies? There has to be a mistake!"

Dr. Graybill shook his head. "I don't think so. We can, of course, order you a more in-depth sonogram later on. In fact, I suggest you go to Santa Fe for additional consultation with a doctor who specializes in multiple births. There will be a lot of things you'll need to know that are a bit different from a standard, single-fetus pregnancy." Dr. Graybill grinned. "Too bad Fiona isn't here. She'd hand you the blue ribbon, Sam."

Seton stared at her husband, feeling the blood drain from her face. Dr. Graybill seemed certain. He'd diagnosed all the other Callahan women in the family with their pregnancies. She doubted he'd made an error. "I can't believe it," she whispered. "My sister is pregnant with only one baby."

Sam gazed at her, looking shaken. "I think we know why you're not having just one. We can probably figure that out, can't we?"

"I saw Dr. Stewart in Santa Fe," Seton told Doc Graybill. "I was taking fertility drugs to give me a boost, because I didn't think I could get pregnant."

"Well, you did just fine, one way or the other." The doctor clapped Sam on the back. "Amazing about you

Callahans. Some of you just seem anxious to have your whole family at once."

Sam looked at Seton again. She could tell he was dumbfounded, and not happy. For that matter, neither was she. Four! She tried to catch her breath.

"You're not going to faint, are you, Seton?" Dr. Graybill asked, and she shook her head.

She wasn't going to faint, but she was certainly worried she was going to wind up with four babies, and minus one husband.

THE TRUCK RIDE HOME with Seton was quiet. Sam's thoughts whirred in his head. Two would have been a shocker. Three babies would have been tough to handle. But four—four!—almost seemed like life was having a good belly laugh at him.

"Damn, Seton," he finally said, "I don't know whether to laugh or cry."

"I know."

She seemed too stunned to say anything else. Sam reached out and put his hand over hers. "Lamb chop, if you're always this efficient, you're going to make me look bad."

She didn't smile the way he'd hoped she would. Sam sighed and turned his attention back to the road. He didn't feel like laughing, either, and the joke had been poorly timed. "I'm sorry," he said.

"No, Sam." Seton sighed. "I'm sorry. This is all my fault."

"Yeah, it is," Sam said, "maybe. I mean, some of my brothers had multiples without a boost." He shrugged. "Maybe those drugs worked and maybe they didn't. We'll never know, so it does no good to regret it. I'll be happy with four sons. I think." He frowned. "That's almost as many as our mom and dad had over several years."

Seton looked out the window, pulling her hand away from his. Sam sighed. They'd work it out.

They had to.

He just wasn't sure how.

"I GUESS I WIN, after all, just like we planned in the very beginning," Sam told his brothers as they sat upstairs in the library, having a weekly meeting. Actually, they weren't meeting as much as trying to absorb Sam's super-huge news. "If there was anything to win, I would. However, since Bode's given up the fight and the ranch has been divided, I get four bundles of joy just because I'm the lucky one in the family."

"Lucky or the best shot," Rafe observed. "That's like one of those pool moves where one ball hits several others and they all sink. Always looks so easy on TV." Rafe grinned at him. "That's kind of what you did, a one-shot multi-pocket, bro."

Judah raised his glass. "I think it's the luck of the baby. We've always known Sam had it easier than the rest of us."

"Easier!" Sam glared at his brothers. "I don't see how four babies is going to be easier, on me or Seton." He shook his head. "The doctor said something about bed rest coming sooner with quadruplets, but I could barely focus on what he was saying. In fact, I think I might have been a little light-headed," he added thoughtfully.

Pete laughed. "That's shock, bro. Every dad gets it. Some worse than others."

Sam shrugged. "I don't know what I'm going to do about my wife."

"What's to do?" Creed asked. "Whether you like it or not, you've been blessed with four babies. In a few days, you'll get excited about it. I think."

Sam wasn't certain. At the moment, he thought his overriding emotion was fear. *Who the hell am I? How can I be a father?*

"Personally, I think it's hellaciously amusing that Seton snuck up on you like that," Judah said. "I remember when you said you weren't going to be caught by a woman, that you weren't going to be a sad sack running after a female. Seton went ahead and pulled the trigger for you, times four."

His brothers laughed. Sam scratched his head, still not sure what he thought about his little wife's plan. "It wasn't supposed to go this way. She and I were just going to get married, no strings attached. Sort of."

"Ha," Pete said, "that'll teach you to try to plot your future. When it comes to wives and babies, it's all about hanging on for dear life."

Yeah, but his brothers were so happy with their wives. Sam wondered if he and Seton would ever get to that stage.

He sort of felt she'd been dishonest, but that wasn't true. She'd never made any secret of how much she wanted a child. "I don't know what I'm going to do," Sam said. "I think I should be mad at her, but I'm pretty certain I'm just freaked out."

"Well," Creed began, in a kindly tone, "too bad there's nothing for you to win anymore. Thanks to Bode, we're free men again."

Sam shrugged and raised his glass when his brothers

did, toasting his news. Part of him knew he should be with Seton at this moment. She had no one to talk to, not really. There was her aunt, and maybe her sister, if Sabrina was around, not to mention four other Callahan brides on the ranch. He sighed. "I better go. I'm pretty sure I should be celebrating with my wife. Not with you laughing hyenas."

That set his brothers off on a great wave of guffaws—*turkeys!*—and so Sam slunk off, not sure how a man who wasn't ready to be a dad could be suddenly expecting quadruplets.

Four little babies who were going to need him.

He had to pull himself together.

Chapter Eleven

"I don't know how to tell you this," Seton said two weeks later, and Sam raised his hands high in the air.

"I surrender," he said. "I don't think I can wrap my poor slow brain around any more of your news bulletins, love."

She shook her head. "Maybe you need another law case to take on. You're sounding out of practice, for the bulldog attorney you're supposed to be."

She smiled as she stared at her computer screen, and Sam took a seat beside her with a deep sigh. "Is this going to work for you as a pseudo-office? We can make more adjustments, but I have a funny feeling you're not going to be going to your office in town much longer. Even I can see that you're growing more bountiful."

"I have a little while longer, I hope," she said, "and this office you put together for me is nice. Thank you, Sam."

This time she smiled at him, and Sam's heart filled up. He was still glad he'd married her, even if she was a tricky little thing. Secretly, he liked the fact that he had to stay on his toes around her. Seton was so sweet and so kind that he hadn't been able to stay disgruntled with her for long.

After all, she hadn't been on the pregnancy medication that long. He'd finally realized that it was probably just plain ol' Callahan testosterone and good fortune that had brought him four babies. And the fact that he'd always known he was more manly than his brothers. If nothing else, he'd decided that finding himself pregnant with multiples had to confirm he was part of the Callahan family tree. He preferred that thought to the alternative, so he was staying with it.

Sam grinned at his wife, who regarded him with suspicion. "I bet those drugs you were taking were about the same as when doctors used to prescribe ketchup and sugar for things. Useless."

She raised a brow. "I'm sure it was all you, cowboy. The fact that I can't zip up any pants I once loved is a testament to your amazing virility."

He nodded, feeling buffered now. "I'm ready to hear your latest bomb, doll."

Seton rolled her eyes, then shook her head. "I can't find any records regarding your parents' deaths. None. I've called several offices in different counties, even checked with some places in Ireland, just in case for some reason their deaths had happened over there, since you boys don't remember. There are no records anywhere."

Sam frowned. "Are records from that many years ago easy to find?"

"Yes." Seton nodded. "Even handwritten death certificates are computerized in most cases, and files are available in all counties. Something should have turned up."

Sam absorbed her statement, puzzling over the implications. "Why would two people—people married to each other—have no traceable records?"

Seton shrugged. "That's a question you'd have to ask Fiona. Possibly they died in such a remote location that records weren't made. The only thought that comes to mind, which would be impossible, is that your parents never died." She looked at Sam with compassion in her eyes. "I'm sorry not to have more concrete information. I'll keep looking."

"Thanks," he said, feeling numb and somehow unsure how to take what he was hearing.

"The only other thought is that your folks weren't who they said they were," Seton said slowly.

Sam grunted. "Which doesn't make sense, because Fiona is definitely our aunt, and though I wasn't born yet, Jonas knows that Fiona was the next of kin. So she came to raise us. Now, come over here and sit in my lap so I can ponder this mystery more fully."

Seton looked at him. "How would that help you think?"

"It's a theory I have. If you're sitting on my lap," Sam said, reaching for her and drawing her to him, "it'll relax me." He put his hands over her stomach, enjoying feeling the roundness where his babies were. "Something about having all five of my babies right here with me has to help the cogs and wheels turn."

Seton relaxed against his chest. "Your cogs and wheels seem to turn pretty quickly, anyway."

"Yeah." He put his face in her hair and nuzzled her neck. "But having you this close helps me think better, I just know it."

"It's helping you do something," Seton said. "I feel like Mount Saint Helens is rising underneath me."

"About that—" Sam said, but Seton fled.

"Nope, that's not thinking," she said, sitting back down at her computer. "And you're paying me to think."

"I'd pay you to sit in my lap and take care of the Mount Saint Helens problem," Sam said, "but you'd probably accuse me of being shallow. Which I am, I must admit." He watched his pretty wife frown at the screen, and realized she was paying zero attention to his attempts to woo her into bed.

"It makes no sense that no one in this town knows what happened to your parents," she mused. "This is not D.C. We're a small community, and everybody is always in each other's business, 24/7."

"Yeah." Sam rubbed at his stubble, and tried to focus on what Seton was saying and not how gorgeous she was with the late-afternoon sun spilling in on her. They probably couldn't have sex much longer, and that alone was going to kill him. "Did I ever tell you how much I enjoy making love with you?"

Seton turned her head and smiled at him. "The feeling is returned, cowboy."

"Any chance—"

"No," Seton said, quashing his hopes. "Because you said you'd think, and you're not."

He closed his eyes, willing himself to concentrate so Seton might favor him with her body. It was a pretty neat trick a woman had, this business of making a man want her so much that he wasn't entirely opposed to going without football, cigar nights with buddies, brawling.... Sam's eyes snapped open. "Bode knows."

She turned to look at him again, her brows arched. "Bode?"

"He has to." Sam's thoughts were running a mile a

minute. "He knows exactly what happened to them. It's why he tried to get our ranch."

"Wait," Seton said. "This isn't making sense."

"No, it's not." Sam stood. "I'm going to go talk to Rafe."

"Why Rafe?"

"Because he's Bode's son-in-law. He's been spending time with the old coot, playing cards and dominoes and sharing a few toots of whiskey from time to time. Rafe's a softie," Sam said, knowing exactly how a man went from being a hard-ass to a softie at the hands of a woman. "He couldn't stand Julie not being on good terms with her dad because of him. Couldn't bear his daughters not knowing their grandfather, even if he is an old fart. Rafe's a thinker," Sam said. "Sometimes he thinks too much. However, in this case, he's probably right."

Seton blinked. "So what does all that mean?"

"It means that Rafe is the one to weasel any information Bode has out of him," Sam said with satisfaction. "I'm going to go explain to my brother what he needs to do."

"And then," Seton said, "tonight I'll reward you for thinking so hard."

Sam smiled. "And I'll reward you for being such a studious P.I. Obviously, you're going to be worth every penny, sweetheart."

He laughed as she shook her head at him, and went off to corner his brother.

"NOT ME," RAFE SAID, when Sam found him in the tack room. "I'm not going to pump my father-in-law. He'll think I've been sucking up to him. And I have been, but for far different reasons. You want your info, you go get it."

"It affects all of us," Sam pointed out.

"Yep," Rafe said, slinging a saddle across a wooden horse for oiling. "And you're the legal beagle married to the gumshoe who thought up this angle. You take care of it. That's why we pay you the big bucks."

"You don't pay me anything," Sam said, and Rafe laughed.

"Well, we got you at the right price then." He whistled as he began rubbing the saddle. "You'll find Bode enjoying his evening meal right about now. Afterward, if you offer him a whiskey, he'll likely not shoot you on sight. Wave the bottle in clear view of the windows when you set foot on his property. That's my advice."

"Great." Sam went off to find a bottle of whiskey—thankfully, Burke kept a generous cellar of necessary libations—and drove next door to Bode's. He held the bottle up over his head and strode to the front door.

"Leave it on the porch!" Bode yelled from inside the house. "And get off my property!"

"I'm not leaving it unless you let me in!" Sam yelled back. Two could play at being crotchety neighbors.

Bode flung open the door. "Why are you bothering me at dinnertime?"

Sam pushed his way in, knowing he wouldn't get a ready invite. "Because I'm hungry, and no one should eat alone, not even you."

Bode muttered what sounded like a curse word—although Sam preferred to think it was just an effusive greeting at his sudden appearance—and led the way into his study. "I know why you're here."

"No, you don't." Sam sat in a leather wingback chair

and relinquished the bottle. "You don't know anything. Quit acting like you do."

"Yeah, I do." Bode begrudgingly handed him a plain glass that looked as if it had been purchased at Walmart. "That's my best crystal. Don't get your paw marks all over it."

"It'll wash." Sam sniffed. "Unlike the marks you'll leave on your glass, Jenkins. The devil doesn't leave anything behind that soap can fix."

"All right," Bode said. "With customary greetings out of the way, you want to talk about why I chose to fold on getting you off your property."

"Well," Sam said, momentarily distracted, "that would be interesting. It's a story you can share with me another day. Right now, I want to hear what happened to our parents. I'm sure you know something, because you mentioned it to Rafe at one point. I filed it in the back of my brain at the time, when you told him to ask Fiona about everything, but it's finally blown out of my mental filing cabinet." Sam raised his glass. "So, let's have it."

"You ain't gonna get it from me," Bode said, staring straight at him, "because I promised your no-good father I wouldn't say a word."

Sam blinked. "My no-good father?"

"That's right. Jeremiah Callahan. Who'd you think your dad was?" Bode glared at him. "You're supposed to be the brains of the outfit."

"No, that's Rafe," Sam murmured. "Sometimes it's Jonas." His gaze shot to Bode's. "But I came after our parents died. How can Jeremiah Callahan be my father?"

Bode looked at him. "How do you think, bright boy? Your mother was pregnant with you. I remember it."

"Jonas said I came later."

"Aw." Bode blew out a breath. "A six-year-old boy doesn't know whether his mother's expecting a baby or not. He just remembers that they left, and one day, you arrived. That's an interesting enough event that even a young kid would marvel at it, sort of like the tooth fairy."

Sam hesitated. "Are you saying Mom didn't die when Fiona said she did?"

Bode remained silent, his eyes glittering.

"That doesn't make sense. If Mom was alive, she'd be here with us. She would never have given us up," Sam said slowly.

Bode took a long drink of whiskey. "Unless she had to. And that's all I'm going to say."

Sam swallowed more spirits himself. The idea that their mother might still be alive tantalized him. He wondered just how cruel the old buzzard, Bode, could be. Sam had never known Molly Callahan. Over the years, he'd hungered for whatever details he could learn about his parents from his brothers and friends in town. "Bode, here's the thing," he said finally. "I don't care what promise you made. You can either tell me now or tell me after I've done you a physical mischief, but trust me when I say that I'll pound your head in if you don't start talking."

"That's against the law," Bode told him, and Sam shrugged.

"We're not in court anymore. Your daughter's not the judge on the case, and she's married to my brother. You want to keep things nice and smooth between our two families, neighbor, because as I understand it, you really like those three little granddaughters of yours."

Bode sighed. "I'm betting your parents are still alive," he said, rocking Sam's entire world, "because they were when they left. But you didn't hear it from me, you heard it from your little fact-finding wife. Or someone else, I don't care who. Maybe you figured it out on your own. More information than that you'll have to dig out of your busybody aunt."

Sam's breath came in gulps. He wanted to believe what Bode was saying, but wasn't sure he could trust him.

"Why would Fiona lie?" He shook his head. "Anyway, everybody in town probably remembers the same thing you do. How can you know what nobody else knows?"

"One—" Bode said, holding up a finger "—and you're really trying my patience here 'cause my TV dinner's getting cold and they only re-warm well once—my dear wife spent a whole lot of time over there helping your mother, especially after she got pregnant with you. Your mom had a helluva case of morning sickness, and with five other boys, she needed help."

Sam knew something about bad morning sickness, because for a while Seton's had lasted what seemed all night and all day. It had worried him sick to see her that miserable, and he'd been racked with guilt that she was suffering so much. "All right, I'm with you so far."

"So my wife knew a bit more than other folks in town. And Fiona showed up one day with Burke, before your parents left. She spent a couple of days with them. My wife said your mother was showing her the ropes about caring for you kids."

Sam blinked. "Dear sweet Jesus, you are a lying son of a bitch." The idea that their parents might have deliberately left them chilled him.

Bode shook his head. "When they left, Fiona cooked up a tale about how your folks had gone on a long summer vacation together, before the new baby was born. Suddenly," Bode said, drawing from his glass, "one day Fiona told folks in town that there'd been a tragic accident. People came rushing to help her and Burke, of course, and they never questioned—or never thought to question—the fact that suddenly Fiona had rearranged the details and was claiming that she was your father's sister." Bode laughed to himself. "I always thought that part was funny as hell. It was the bit that set off the alarm bells for me. I knew why she did it, of course. She wanted to bury the trail. Only we knew Fiona was really Molly's sister, because my wife had spent so much time over at their place."

"What trail?" Sam demanded.

"As I figure it, the trail leading to your parents." Bode handed his glass over for a refill, and Sam poured generously.

"You tell one hell of a crazy tale, old man."

Bode laughed, not taking offense. "It's only crazy because of your aunt. Trust me, if anyone ever needed someone to cover their ass, their hide and their whereabouts, she's the one to do it. I've never known a woman for such plotting."

Now that, Sam knew, was a true statement.

"My wife swore me to secrecy, of course, because she was an angel," Bode said, reminiscing, his TV dinner forgotten. "She didn't want any harm to come to your aunt and you boys. I made that promise, and I kept it, until today."

His eyes gleamed at Sam over the glass. "I knew one of you would come asking someday. I thought you had to start figuring things out. When you didn't, I decided I might as well have your ranch. I figured I could beat Fiona. It should have been mine, anyway, but the Navajos considered your father family, even though he was from a different tribe. I don't know which one."

Bode set his glass down and crossed his arms over his chest. "I also underestimated you boys' survival instincts. You put on a helluva court case, and I don't mind saying getting my daughter knocked up was brilliant." The older man shrugged. "Once Julie told me she was pregnant, I knew the game was up. You boys inherited your aunt's skills."

"Rafe did not get Julie pregnant on purpose," Sam said, irritated as hell.

His neighbor laughed. "It doesn't matter anymore. You're right. Those three granddaughters of mine are my wife come back to me, and I'm not about to screw up anything, even if that means sharing a drink now and again with you. Now get out, and next time, don't bring the cheap stuff."

"Cheap!" Sam glanced at the bottle. "You old buzzard, that's some of Kentucky's finest you put in that cheap glass you probably got at a gas station."

Bode sniffed. "I prefer Crown Royal. Remember that the next time you want something from me."

Sam stared at Bode, watching him close his eyes and prepare—or pretend—to nap. It was a fantastic fairy tale the old man told.

The old jackass didn't have a reason to lie anymore.

As he said, he'd do anything to keep on good terms, because now his goals had changed. Instead of their ranch, he was focused on little Janet, Julianne and Judith.

It didn't matter. Sam had gotten a lot of what he'd come for.

He stood. "Thanks, Bode. It's a pleasure keeping neighborly relations so neighborly."

The old man shrugged. "I'll deny it if you ever breathe my name concerning anything you heard here today."

"Don't worry. No one would believe me." Sam left, his mind whirling, his whole body tense as a guitar string. How? How could what Bode was saying be true?

But it made perfect sense. It explained so much—and now Sam knew.

He was one of the Callahans. He was family.

He belonged.

Chapter Twelve

Sam took a day to mull over what he'd learned, then decided not to think too hard about it anymore. They'd probably never know the whole truth, and he had more important things on his mind at the moment.

Like his wife.

"So that's what you dug up, gorgeous," Sam said as he finished relating his adventure with Bode to her. He cast an appreciative eye over Seton. There was something to be said for having a wife who knew how to find answers. "Why are you all dressed up? Did I miss a doctor's appointment?"

Seton smiled. She pulled him from the bunkhouse kitchen, where Sam had found her, and led him down the hall. He thought she was going in the right direction if she had in mind what he had on his.

"That can't be all of the story," Seton said. "There are too many questions. Such as what *did* happen to your parents?"

Sam grabbed his wife, halting her as he realized she was about to take a wrong turn into a room that wasn't their bedroom. "That's Jonas's problem. I've done all the work for this lazy family that I intend to." He tugged her close to him and gave her a thorough kissing. "I feel like a weight has been lifted off of me. A weight the size of a horse."

Seton touched his face for just a second with her cool, gentle hand. God, he loved the feel of this woman, especially round and cutely plump as she was becoming. "I'm glad you're happy."

"Remember when I told you I didn't know who I was?" Sam asked.

She nodded. "I knew who you were, though."

"So you said." He planted a kiss on her nose and tried to edge her a little closer to the bedroom. For some reason, he thought he detected a wee bit of reluctance on her part to be led astray for some early-evening romance. "But now I know who I am, and it changes everything for me. Although I'm not exactly swallowing Bode's entire tale, he did seem pretty definitive about a lot of details that make sense."

His wife smiled at him. "I told you Mr. Jenkins wasn't the bogeyman you boys made him out to be. He's got his good side, too."

"No, he doesn't. He tried to work me over for better liquor. Trust me, for a man who won't part with a penny, he sure does like his spirits to be of the finest quality. Why do you keep trying to get me into another room besides the one I know you know I'm trying to take you to? Has my evening with Bode left a stench on me?"

"No." Seton laughed. "Are you sure you're through with all your news?"

"Yes." Realizing their dance wasn't getting him toward the bedroom, he settled for running his hands over his wife's derriere. "As I said, Jonas is in Ireland hunting for the redoubtable aunt and uncle. Once he finds them, he can lay Bode's story on them. I've given the pertinent details to my brothers, and they're as stunned as I am, and last I saw, trying to figure out if Bode was trying to mess with our heads." Sam grinned. "My gut tells me he likes those little grandbabies of his too much to try any shenanigans at this point."

"I'm sure you're right." Seton took a deep breath. "All right, if you're done with your news for the moment, because I have a feeling this will be a developing story," she said with a smile, "I have something to show you."

"Will you be naked?" Sam asked hopefully. "I wouldn't mind seeing you nude, if you care to take a hint, wife."

Seton laughed and pushed open the door to a room Sam realized had been made over into a nursery. "Holy smokes," he said, his gaze going at once to the four white cribs—four of everything—centered in the room. "What have you been doing while I was gone? Turning this place into a baby factory?"

Seton looked at him proudly. "My sisters-in-law and sister gave me—us—a baby shower."

He blinked. "Did they ever. We're going to be showered with babies, and snowed under baby crapola." His heart thundered as the visual reality hit him. "This is actually happening. We're going to have four babies."

Seton laughed again. "Yes, Sam. Isn't this a fabulous nursery?"

"I guess so." He gazed around at all the stuff. "Good thing we moved into the bunkhouse. I think it's the only property we own with a room big enough to hold four babies at once."

"I know." Seton went over and turned on a motor-ized swing, setting a pink-and-white bear sitting in it rocking. "Almost everything in here is hand-me-downs from the other Callahan babies."

Sam considered the stuffed animal with a frown. "Good. Because my boys aren't going to play with pink bears." There were four of them, in four matching swings, but only one bear was getting a ride. The other three sat with equally content smiles on their faces. Sam felt a little sweat start under his hatband. "It's a lot of stuff, Seton."

"Yes." She laughed at him again. Sam knew his face was frozen, and he couldn't seem to relax his muscles. "Anyway, the doctor hasn't said we're having boys, Sam."

"It's about time one of us Callahans did. We're going to be having weddings around here until someone finally decides to rename our ranch Rancho Wedding-O."

"No." Seton gently tugged him over to a small settee and curled up in his lap when he collapsed. "And I have more news."

Sam's head was already spinning. "Please don't tell me the doctor discovered a fifth taking up space in your tiny little stomach. Seriously, Seton, I don't know how you're going to hold four babies. You're a little taller than some ladies, but you're thin." He looked at her expanding stomach with some concern.

Seton nodded. "As always, husband, you're on the case. I had my appointment today, and the doctor says I'm on bed rest."

He blinked. "Is everything all right? Do you feel okay? How come I didn't know you had an appointment?" He glared at her, not happy that she'd left him out of something important.

She ran a soothing hand down his arm as she nestled against his chest. "First, you had your own important errands to take care of. Second, you don't have to go to the doctor with me every time, Sam. It's boring. You're sweet to want to, though."

"It's not boring with those kinds of news bulletins." Sam regarded his wife unhappily. "So if you're on bed rest, why did you have a baby shower? I'm sure it was more excitement than you needed."

"It was a surprise shower," Seton said. "They didn't tell you because they said you'd be underfoot if you knew, and I think your sisters-in-law might be right about you." She gave him a considering look. "You are a bit of a control freak."

"Oh, brother." Sam closed his eyes, enjoying the feel of his wife in his lap. She was all curves and soft skin, and he loved holding her. "Wait," he said, his eyes flashing open. "Does bed rest mean resting and nothing else in bed?"

She giggled. "I'm afraid so."

Damn. He had a situation of epic proportions in his jeans right at this moment, courtesy of his warm, sweet wife sitting in his lap. Sam groaned. "These four little sons of mine are selfish."

"For the next few months, I guess so." Seton kissed him on the cheek, then on the lips, and whispered, "But I still think we should celebrate your big news."

"Which big news?" Sam asked. "I don't know which news is biggest. It's all changed my life."

"Let's celebrate it all," she said, and Sam felt her cool, smooth hand reach into his jeans.

Maybe this bed rest thing wasn't going to be as awful as it sounded.

"THIS BED REST THING is terrible," Sam told Seton the next day. "I hate leaving you here. I know you have to be bored. And I don't like the term 'high-risk pregnancy.' You said nothing about high risk when you lured me into a sexual adventure yesterday."

Seton smiled from where she lay on the sofa. He tried to think if she had everything she needed within reach. The worry was going to kill him.

"It wasn't a sexual adventure, Sam, honestly. I've put more effort into whisking eggs." She gave him a teasing wink.

Sam sighed. His wife did have quite an effect on him. She'd been growing on his heart ever since the day he'd proposed to her and realized he was really just looking for an excuse to tie Seton to him forever. "Don't remind me. The more I have you, the more I want you."

"Good. Now just hold that thought for another four months or so."

Sam felt himself go pale. Literally felt blood rush from his head. "Four plus three equals only seven months, Seton."

"I'll be lucky if I go seven months, probably. That's why it's called a high-risk pregnancy, Sam."

He staggered to the end of the sofa to sit beside her. "You're going to stay totally still and not move a muscle until the doctor says you can. I'll have Banger's bring by food every night."

"Our generous sisters-in-law said they'd take care of your garbage bin of a gut. Everything is going to be fine. Where's my nerves-of-steel guy who strikes fear into the meanest hearts in the courtroom?"

"Gone," Sam said with a groan. "Finished off. A shadow of his former self."

"What a wienie," Seton said with a laugh. "Go on, please. I'm trying to figure out how to knit a bootie. Today is knitting day, you know. Some ladies are coming to teach me, so don't lock the door on your way out."

Sam kissed her goodbye, not certain she should even be knitting. Not knowing what to do with himself, he made his way out into the sunshine.

And then, like a mirage, he saw the mystical black Diablos running, their hooves flying as they galloped across the horizon toward the east.

And Sam knew something was about to happen.

Chapter Thirteen

"So it looks like neither one of us will ever wear the magic wedding dress," Seton told Corinne a week later, when her aunt came out to the ranch to visit and check on the knitting process. "I didn't want to wear it, because Sam and I were getting married under false pretenses. And Sabrina and Jonas will never get to the altar."

Corinne sat on the leather sofa across from the one Seton had taken over. Sam had practically set up a command center for her, with two cell phones, drinks, food, tissues—it looked like a small convenience store—on a nearby table. Corinne eyed all the items and smiled at her niece.

"Let's tackle the last worry first. Jonas and Sabrina might find their way to the altar. Your mother's wedding dress may get worn by one of her daughters. It's not totally hopeless."

"It's not really Mom's," Seton said. "She got the dress from a lady somewhere in Upper Bavaria, where she was from, who claimed that the gown had been worn by someone important, like a duchess or something. I don't really remember the story. Anyway, it was supposed to have some kind of magical properties. Jackie,

Aberdeen, Darla and Julie all claim that when they put on the dress, they knew exactly who the right man for them was."

Corinne smiled. "Around here, we enjoy tales of mysticism. I wouldn't give up on getting Sabrina into the gown. Now, what do you mean, you and Sam married under false pretenses?"

Seton glanced at the door to make certain no other visitors—or her husband—were about to pop in. "Sam and I knew that Sabrina was never coming back, because she was pregnant with Jonas's baby and didn't want him to know. So we cooked up this idea that if we had a pretend engagement party, or even a pretend wedding, she'd probably come home. We went with getting married for real, because at the time, Sam was still thinking about Fiona's stipulation that the men be married to get their part of the ranch. Only then," Seton said, taking a deep breath, "Sam got notified at the altar that Bode was giving up the fight for the ranch. So that basically nullified Fiona's stipulation. There was no longer a rush to divide the ranch up to try to keep Bode from being able to take it."

"But Sam wanted to marry you, anyway," Corinne said.

Seton nodded. "Which confused me at the time, because we'd already gotten Sabrina home, and goodness knows, that went over like a popped balloon. Jonas and Sabrina probably didn't say three words to each other. And Sam and I knew we'd made everything worse."

Her aunt's eyes twinkled. "I do seem to remember that they didn't have a lot to say to one another."

"And Jonas left right after the wedding, as if he'd been shot out of a canon. Neither Sam nor I realized until later that his brother was such a dunderhead he never considered that maybe Sabrina is carrying his child."

"I can see where the mistake could be made," Corinne said. "Sabrina had been gone for months. And she didn't bother to inform him, even though anyone who knows Sabrina knows she's a fairly direct lady. So I can see how the misunderstanding could develop."

"Yes." Seton was so sad for her sister. "She just doesn't want Jonas to feel he's stuck with her, since they never had a real relationship, or so she claims. I'm pretty certain Jonas was crazy about her. In fact, now that we know he can't find Fiona and Burke, but still hasn't come home, I think he's off nursing a broken heart."

"What does Sam say?"

"Sam says—" Seton glanced toward the door once again "—that Jonas is a lightweight in the love department. That Jonas, the great heart doctor, can't take even so much as a scratch on his own four-chambered ventricular muscle. That was how my windbag of a husband put it."

Corinne giggled. "Well, I think Sam's overstating it a bit. All Jonas knows is that Sabrina is expecting a child."

"Yeah. It seems we made everything worse." Seton looked at her aunt. "And I've made everything worse for me and Sam. He acts so happy right now that it makes me nervous. Because I know he didn't want a child, and now he's having four. He didn't really want anything, except to get Sabrina and Jonas together."

"And yet here you are!" Corinne said cheerfully. "With so many things happening, one just has to believe it's all meant to be! Let me get you a glass of water. This July is going to be one of the hottest on record."

"Thank you." Seton accepted the water her aunt handed her, even though she wasn't thirsty. "I wish I didn't have this uneasy feeling that Sam's acting happy just because he feels there's nothing else he can do."

Her aunt shrugged. "He didn't have to marry you. It seems he wanted to. And he seems to like you well enough, or you wouldn't be in a family way." She smiled at Seton. "The difference between you and Sam, and Jonas and Sabrina, is that you and Sam went ahead and jumped in with both feet. No fear."

"I'm afraid," Seton said. "I'm very afraid. I want my husband to be happy." Actually, she wanted Sam to be in love with her, the way she was with him. "I feel strangely like I trapped him, Aunt Corinne."

"Because you wanted a baby."

Seton nodded. "Yes. Mind you, I didn't think anything would happen quite so soon...."

"You're worried about nothing, I really do think." Corinne arranged some cookies on a tray and some fruit beside them. "Sam's a grown man. He knows how babies are made, Seton. If you're worried that you don't have your husband's heart, it might be due to something else."

Seton didn't know whether she had Sam's heart or not, that was true. He seemed happy, but it had all happened so fast.... "I don't think I expected to fall in love with him quite as hard as I have," she admitted. "I came back here to find out if there could ever be anything between us—"

"And now that there is, you're not certain it can be real." Corinne smiled at her. "Try not to worry so much, dear. No one dragged Sam to the altar. I was there, and as I recall, he was more interested in being wed than you were."

Seton smiled. "That surprised me, too."

"Well, then. Don't borrow trouble. That would be my advice."

"And worth taking, I might add," Sam said, coming out of the back bedroom. Seton gasped, shocked by her husband's sudden appearance.

"Sam! I thought you were out on the ranch!"

"I was. I came in the back, trying to be quiet so I wouldn't awaken my turtledove, who's supposed to be getting her twenty-four hours of beauty rest." He came over and kissed her on the forehead, then gave her aunt a hug. "Thanks for keeping an eye on her, Corinne. She's going a little stir-crazy." He gave Seton a concerned glance. "I'm not sure how I'm going to keep her on this sofa for another five months."

"Sam," Seton said slowly, "there's something I have to tell you."

Her aunt stood. "I should be going."

Sam glanced from one to the other. "That's not good, if Corinne doesn't want to hang around to hear your news."

Seton sighed. "Corinne, stay, do."

"Well," she said, and Sam sat down next to where she had been, and patted the seat beside him. "All right, just for a moment or two."

"Let's have it, wife."

Seton looked at Corinne, who knew what she was about to say. Then she took a deep breath. "Sam, you know Corinne took me for my checkup today."

"Yes, I do." Sam beamed. "Usually, I'm on board for

the checkup, Corinne, but today was a big day at the ranch. Thanks for filling in."

"Well," Seton said, wanting to get her news out quickly, "today was one of the umpteen sonograms I have to have as a high-risk pregnancy—"

"I hate that term. I prefer to think of it as high-value," Sam said.

"And Sam," Seton said, trying not to let him stop her flow, "we're having four girls."

Sam's jaw dropped. "Four...girls?"

Corinne laughed at his expression. Even Seton had to smile, he looked so dumbstruck.

"Four girls?" he repeated.

"Yes," Seton said, "and so far, everything seems to be healthy and fine."

"That's great. That's great!" Sam exclaimed. He hopped up to give his wife a kiss on the forehead, then headed to the door. "I'm going to go tell my brothers the good news. I'll be back in a little while."

He went out, and they could him whistling as he walked.

"Do you see what I mean?" Seton asked.

"Too happy," Corinne said. "Maybe he really is."

"But all he's talked about is having boys."

"They all do," her aunt said wisely, "but there's something about 'Daddy's little girls' that steals a man's heart. All the Callahan men dote on their daughters. I think it's because there were six of those rascal boys growing up that makes them enjoy the lace and frills and my-daddy's-a-hero of little girls."

"I hope you're right," Seton said. "I'm starting to get worried. Sam's always just so happy."

"You know," Corinne said, "it may be that the man is in love."

Seton blinked. "He hasn't said so."

Her aunt smiled and stood. "Time will tell. For now, just relax and enjoy the bliss of being pregnant. Try to trust him just a little. Sam's a pretty smart guy. He knew what he was doing, I believe."

Seton smiled, then sighed when he popped back into the den. "Yes, Sam?"

He looked at her. "Seton, how long does the doctor think we have until the babies are born?"

"Maybe another couple of months, if everything goes well," she said, and Sam groaned.

"I'm going to hire a nurse for you," he said. "Someone who can be with you around the clock, instead of all our family and friends."

"Sam, I don't want a nurse," Seton said. "If I need a nurse, can't Darla or Jackie come by sometimes?"

He shook his head. "I need a nurse who's experienced in multiple births. Never mind, I'll get this figured out."

He disappeared again, and Seton turned to Corinne. "Did you see that?"

"Yes," she said with a laugh. "If you were worried about him being too happy and not really expressing his true feelings, I think you just sampled them."

"But I don't need a nurse," Seton stated.

Corinne picked up her handbag. "Welcome to the new Sam. I think you'll be getting a nurse, until he decides to hire two."

"Oh, for heaven's sake," Seton exclaimed. "He's going to have to calm down."

"All the Callahan men were like this," Corinne said. "I think you've just seen the last of Serene Sam."

"Argh," Seton said, wishing she had the worry-free Sam back.

But she had some worries, too.

Since the next day was "Sabrina's Day" to look after her, Seton was ready to have the talk with her sister she felt she should have had long before. "The problem," she told Sabrina, "is that you're here keeping an eye on me, when someone should be keeping an eye on you. You're further along than I am," she added, with an amazed glance at her sister's growing stomach.

"I'm fine," Sabrina said. "I have only one baby to think about, who seems to sleep most of the day and night so far."

"Not mine," Seton said wryly. "They feel like they're a mosh pit at a concert, always moving, although the doctor says they don't have hardly any room left in there. I have to go to the bathroom about every thirty minutes, so it's a good thing we're in the bunkhouse, Sam says. Plenty of bathrooms."

Sabrina laughed. "It's fun expecting together."

"Yeah." Seton wasn't having much fun—she felt glued to the sofa during the day—but she wasn't complaining. She wanted the babies to know that she loved them, and wanted them to stay in as long as they possibly could. "Speaking of being pregnant together, there's something I have to tell you."

Sabrina smiled at her. "I hope you're going to tell me that you and Sam have decided you're wildly in love with each other."

"Not yet. I mean, we're definitely happy. And I know I did the right thing by marrying Sam." Seton looked at her beautiful sister, wishing Sabrina could have as much happiness with Jonas as Seton was finding with Sam—unexpected as that was. "I'm definitely falling in love with him."

Sabrina smiled. "That's the best news I've heard lately, besides the fact that I'm going to be aunt to four lovely girls."

"Thank you." Seton gazed at her, knowing that the moment had come. "But that brings me to something I need to tell you, Sabrina."

"There's a fifth baby I'll be aunt to?" Sabrina asked.

"Poor Sam if there were," she exclaimed, and they both laughed. "No," Seton said after a pensive moment, "what I want to tell you is that Sam and I planned our wedding so that you'd come home."

Sabrina looked at her. "I'm glad I came back to Diablo now. Is that what's been bothering you—that you think you dragged me home?"

"No, I mean we actually planned a wedding drama, a sort of one-act play, to get you home. So you'd see Jonas, and he'd see you, and hopefully realize—"

"Oh," Sabrina said. "I see where you're going with this. But are you telling me that you and Sam wouldn't have gotten married if I hadn't been pregnant?"

"Well, we certainly wouldn't have thought of it, I don't believe," Seton said, although she wasn't certain about that anymore, either. She and Sam felt like such a perfect fit it was hard to believe they might not have ever gotten together. "Maybe we were just looking for a reason to get serious."

"Okay," Sabrina said, "so what's the big deal? You're happy, aren't you?"

"Yes, I think we are. But you're not, and that pains me. I feel I hurt you—in fact, I know I did. Because we pushed you and Jonas together, and you guys weren't ready, and now he's gone."

Her sister shrugged. "Although I realize you feel your plan went astray and you messed things up for me, I have to point out that Jonas and I didn't have anything, anyway."

"I don't know. It just seems that we made everything worse."

"Not likely," Sabrina said drily. "But if you're looking for forgiveness, I can honestly tell you that you've got it. I don't care about Jonas, or what he thinks. If he doesn't want any part of this baby's life, that's something I'll deal with."

Seton winced. "I don't think he didn't want any part of your baby's life. I believe, if I understood Sam correctly, that he doesn't think you're having his baby."

"Well, then he's dumb," Sabrina said. "Ugh, don't talk to me any more about Jonas Callahan. Let's just talk about you. That's much more important. And how harebrained was it to fake an engagement just to get me home? What happens if Sam decides he wants a divorce after the babies are born?"

Seton swallowed hard. "I've thought about that. Deceit isn't a good foundation for a marriage, and I've had my share of secrets."

"I wouldn't worry about that," Sabrina said. "Sam's used to secrets at Rancho Diablo. Fiona raised those boys on secrets. Sam likely thinks a plotting female is normal. And maybe even a blessing, because those boys love their aunt, that's for certain."

Seton shook her head. "I don't know. I just keep waiting for the shoe to drop. The one that has my name on it, and the message 'everything was going along too smoothly to be real.'"

"Well," Sabrina said, "at least you're married. The father of my child might not even be in the country when the stork arrives."

Seton didn't think Jonas had any plans to return, not anytime soon. "He wouldn't have left if Sam and I hadn't dreamed up this stupid plan. And I hurt you, as much as you're trying to make me feel that I didn't."

"There's no apology necessary," Sabrina insisted. "The plan worked for you, so that's the good part. If things were meant to work out for me and Jonas, they would have, no matter how much scheming anyone did."

"I guess so," Seton said, aware that her sister was still trying to absolve her of any guilt. "Are you having a boy or a girl?"

Sabrina smiled. "I have no intention of finding out until the big day. I want to be just as surprised as everyone else. But odds are on a girl, considering the boom in pink at the ranch, don't you think?"

The sisters laughed. It was funny how such testosterone-laden men, who prided themselves on being tough guys, were now holding pink-wrapped bundles and lugging around pink-and-white diaper bags—and were so happy about it.

At the same time, Seton couldn't help thinking that it wasn't fair Sabrina would be the only one without her own Callahan man at her side.

Unless Sam changes his mind about us, Seton thought.

Surely four sweet little babies wouldn't make a man run for the hills.

Chapter Fourteen

Around the middle of October, when the sun was turning more copper than golden over Rancho Diablo, Sabrina went into labor.

"Where is Jonas?" Sam growled, running around the bunkhouse as if it were his own child that was being born. "He should be here!"

Seton wanted more than anything to be at the hospital with her sister—and for her husband to calm down. "Jonas isn't here because he doesn't know Sabrina's having his child."

"Well, I'm going to tell him. When I can reach him." Sam started punching numbers into his cell phone, and Seton said, "Sam, stop. We've meddled enough, and Sabrina doesn't want him to know."

Sam reluctantly put his phone away. "I'm going to punch him in the nose when I see him."

Seton looked fondly at her handsome, stressed husband. "Sam, we did our part. It backfired. We're staying out of it from here on."

He sank onto the sofa next to her, absently rubbing her feet. "You're right. As usual."

"Remember that when it's your turn in a few weeks."

Sam glanced at her. "I can't believe there are really four babies inside that belly of yours."

"I believe it." Seton shifted with a slight groan. "I'm glued to this sofa, and I'm so full of drugs to keep these children in that I'm beginning to feel like a slug. I can barely remember what my toes look like."

"Toes are overrated, anyway. I'm much more interested in your breasts, for example."

But Seton couldn't laugh at his attempt at playful husband humor. She was too worried about Sabrina. "Has no one heard from Jonas at all?"

Sam shook his head. "His cell phone no longer accepts messages. I don't know if that's because it's a different country, or what's going on." A frown crossed his face. "This journey of his has nothing to do with finding Fiona and Burke. It's about Jonas finding himself."

"Well, that doesn't sound so bad. Let's just hope he succeeds, and then everyone will be better off."

"When does the nurse come by to check you out?"

"This afternoon. I'll be curious to hear what she says. Last week there was a little concern over my blood pressure."

Sam grunted. "We're all getting high blood pressure around here. Maybe I'll just grab that sofa over there and we'll lie here together and wait for babies."

Seton didn't think Sam could stay still for more than five minutes. He fidgeted like a grasshopper these days. "In a year, we're going to look back on all this and laugh."

He glanced at her. "I'm never going to laugh. I'm too worried about you and my babies and my stupid brother."

She smiled at her husband. It was true that Sam did

seem to be doing his share of sympathetic pregnancy suffering. His hair stood up in a perpetual flag of worry because he was constantly shoving his fingers through it now. "What happened to the young-gun lawyer who laughed in the face of danger?"

Sam sagged onto the sofa opposite hers and grinned. "Long gone, beautiful."

She didn't feel beautiful, but when he flashed that devil-may-care smile at her, she felt she still had some of what Sam had seemed to like so much in the beginning.

Although it was very hard to believe he could fall in love with her when she felt—and looked—like a beached whale. *I'm so in love with him,* Seton realized. *I must have been when I came back to town.*

"I'm going to run to the hospital and see Sabrina," Sam said, standing suddenly. "If my big dumb brother isn't going to be here to do delivery room duty, then I'll step up. I could probably use the practice."

Seton's heart filled to the top with love. "Thank you for helping my sister and going in my place."

He leaned over and kissed her on the lips. "You stay right here on this tuffet, gorgeous, and when I come back, I'll bring pictures of the new branch of your family tree."

AFTER SAM LEFT, Seton opened up the secret journal she'd begun keeping after learning she'd be confined to daily bed rest.

165th day of bed rest. Completely tired, but so excited because Sabrina is having her baby. Wish I could shop for a baby present! Sam sweetly got

*me some gizmo so I can shop online and check
email, but there's something about picking out
baby clothes in person that speaks to me.*

*On our last visit to the doctor, we learned the
babies can now breathe on their own, if absolutely
necessary. They have tiny eyelashes. Surprising
enough, all the girls seem to be healthy—though
tiny!*

*I'm so happy that Sabrina and I will have chil-
dren the same age. Even though we didn't plan
this, it's really a dream come true.*

Everything has been a dream.

Seton closed the journal, stuffing it back between the
sofa cushions where she kept it. Chronicling her pregnancy had given her a timeline to go back and chart the
babies' progress.

The end was in sight.

But what would Sam think about four babies once
they were born? She wondered if he'd ever really for-
given her for not telling him that she was taking fertility drugs.

The bunkhouse door swung open, and Seton pushed
herself up to see who today's visitor was. She blinked,
too astonished to say anything for a moment. "I know
who you are," she said slowly. "You're Chief Running
Bear."

The elderly Native American smiled, his face leath-
ery and kind. "And you're Seton, sister to Sabrina, niece
to Corinne Abernathy, and Fiona's trusted secret-keeper.
You can call me Bear. Or Chief."

Seton hesitated. "I'm not a secret-keeper, or whatever
you just said." She gestured across the coffee table to

the sofa Sam commandeered when he was in the bunkhouse. "Won't you sit down, Chief?"

He sat, smiling the whole time. Seton wondered if
he was always this happy. She felt cheered just looking
at him.

"How do you feel?" he asked.

"Like a moose. But a happy moose, most of the
time. I'm sorry I can't get up to offer you something to
drink—"

He put up a hand. "We will talk this visit."

"All right." Seton nodded, realizing that her chatter didn't mask her nervousness. Secret-keeper? Sam
had called her secretive. She wasn't—at least she didn't
think she was, more than anybody else was. "I'm listening."

He nodded. "In the beginning, when Fiona hired you
and Sabrina to tell the Callahan brothers that the ranch
was in trouble, and that they needed to get married and
have children, you did that for her."

"I didn't," Seton said. "Sabrina did her fortune-teller
thing. I stayed on the sidelines for that act."

"But you never revealed, not even to your husband,
that you'd been hired by Fiona to tell the story she
wanted told."

Seton shifted uncomfortably. "It didn't seem important to bring up."

He smiled again. "You keep secrets well."

"I didn't mean to keep that secret from Sam, or
anyone. It was really Fiona's tale to tell the brothers, not
mine." Seton looked at the chief, who watched her with
black eyes rimmed by laugh lines. "If Sabrina wants
to tell Jonas what she did, that's her choice. I truly had
nothing to do with it."

Perhaps she'd played a supportive role, by being a listening ear. Seton raised her chin, wondering what the chief's point was in bringing up the subject.

It was past history, and she didn't think Jonas—or Sam—should be reminded that she and her sister had started this entire race-for-the-ranch wife-and-baby hunt with Sabrina's charade.

Seton didn't need anything else coming between her and Sam.

The chief seemed unbothered by her claim. "So then Sam asked you to check on his family history."

She wondered how Running Bear knew this. "I might have," she said casually. "Simple stuff that anyone could have found."

He eyed her calmly. "You're still looking."

"Sam said I didn't need to find anything else out. He said he was satisfied knowing that he was part of the family."

"But you're looking."

Seton swallowed. "How do you know?"

The chief gazed at her knowingly. "There are many secrets at Rancho Diablo."

She raised an eyebrow. "That's not a news flash."

"And those secrets must stay hidden."

Her skin went chilly. "Are you still talking about Sam?"

"The Callahan family." He waved a hand in the air to signify the entire clan. "What you know about them must remain known only by you."

"All right," Seton said. "First you tell me how you know I've been looking into the Callahan history, and then I'll tell you what I know. It isn't much."

"You suspect about Jeremiah and Molly," Running

Bear said. "But you won't tell your husband. Or anyone. Not even your sister."

Seton took a deep breath. "You're not going to say how you know this, are you?"

The chief stood. "That is not important. Right now, you should be resting. You have four small miracles who are waiting for you."

She looked up at him. "Waiting for me to do what?"

"To be the guardian to their future. Sam was the last child of her own Molly ever held. She wants her grandchildren to be loved."

"Wants?" Seton repeated quickly. "Then I'm right!"

His gaze stabbed her. "You've been entrusted with the secret. And you will keep it. Everything hinges on your ability to know the right moment to reveal it."

Again cool prickles dotted Seton's arms. "Shouldn't that be your job? Or Fiona's? Why don't you just tell Sam the truth? Tell all the Callahans the truth?"

"It's not safe. The future depends on your willingness to keep the secret. Grave things could happen if everything is revealed before it is time."

The old man's eyes held hers. Seton gasped. "*That's* why Fiona left! It wasn't because of Bode at all. She's protecting the Callahans from knowing the truth, and she was afraid they were starting to ask questions."

The chief didn't answer. He planted his hat firmly over his braided hair, then placed a light hand against her stomach for a moment. "These children are blessed," he said, and departed.

Seton swallowed, staring after the chief. He'd left as quietly and quickly as he'd arrived. She felt as if he'd left a blessing, a benediction, on her children. A faint fragrance of leather and perhaps tobacco lingered, a comforting, grandfatherly scent. Her thoughts raced. How could he possibly have known she was still searching through Sam's family records, trying to find out what had really happened to Molly and Jeremiah, and where their graves were?

The chief was right about one thing: Seton hadn't told Sam what she'd learned. He'd said she didn't need to look anymore, that she'd found out all he needed to know: that he was a true Callahan.

But she was curious, always too curious. The chief was right—she was a secret-keeper.

It was probably going to get her in a lot of trouble one day.

But if the chief wanted her lips sealed, then sealed they would stay. Although it didn't seem right to keep something this important from Sam, when she'd vowed there'd be no more secrets between them.

Seton put a palm on her stomach, feeling her babies move, almost as if something had awakened them from their nap. "Chief Running Bear says you're blessed, babies," she murmured, and hoped the chief knew what he was talking about.

EIGHT HOURS LATER, Sam presented Seton with a picture of her nephew. "Look at that full head of black hair," Sam said proudly. "You get that only with a Callahan. Practically full-grown right at the start!"

Seton giggled at Sam's crowing. "Tell me everything," she demanded, drinking in the photo hungrily. "Blue eyes, dark hair, and I can see a good squall coming out of that mouth—definitely Callahan features."

"You better believe it. We rely on our ability to make

noise," Sam said, lounging next to her to stare at the baby picture. "That's the birth photo that they take a few moments after the baby's been cleaned up and weighed and all that jazz. But Uncle Sam took candids," he said proudly, "so I've got all the good stuff." He placed his camera on the coffee table and put a hand on her stomach, right where the chief had placed his. Seton shot Sam a guilty look.

"And I'm bushed," he said. "You have no idea how hard being a birth coach is."

"You were birth coach?" She couldn't believe Sabrina would allow Sam to be with her. Seton loved him all the more for it.

"I was, and it was great. Sabrina didn't think she needed a coach, but after she got to about eight centimeters, I think she decided any Callahan was better than no Callahan, damn Jonas and his self-discovery tour." Sam frowned. "I'm supposed to be the rabbit-footed wanderer in the family. I really don't appreciate Jonas deciding he's just going to go off and ride the rails during his midlife crisis."

Seton couldn't help smiling at Sam's displeasure with his brother. "Thank you for being with Sabrina. I wish I could have been with her, too."

Sam kissed her on the stomach. "No doubt Sabrina would have preferred to have you, but she got me, and trust me, I discharged my responsibility with utmost detail. I even got ice chips for her."

"That's very good, Sam," Seton said. "So you feel in shape to do it again next week?"

He went pale. "Next week?"

"I'm at thirty-one weeks now and holding steady. But

the doctor says I can't go much longer because of my blood pressure."

Sam's face fell. "They'll be so small."

She nodded. "Probably about two and a half pounds, each, if we're lucky. They're around two pounds now."

He leaned back. "I'd better go over the list one more time with the ladies."

"List?"

"Your aunt and Mavis Night set up a rotating schedule with Jackie, Darla, Aberdeen and Julie, as well as various members of the Books'n'Bingo Society and anybody else who wanted a place on the calendar. Many hands make light work, Corinne said. Don't worry, they have Sabrina in rotation, too. She'll have plenty of help. You McKinley women are prolific."

Seton felt warmed by all the people who wanted to help. "It's great living in Diablo."

"Aren't you glad now you came back?" Sam asked, his head lolling so he could look at her.

And you're the reason I'm here. I just don't know if you'll ever feel the same about me as I do about you.

"Sure," Seton said, "Diablo is wonderful."

He picked up her hand and held it to his lips for a moment. "Everything is going to be fine."

She gazed at her husband and tried to smile. "Thanks again for being with Sabrina."

His eyelids began to drift shut. She could see how worn-out Sam was from his big day as birth coach. "This week the tiny redhead, next week the big blonde. Babies, babies, babies."

She punched him in the arm, and his eyes flew open. "I was not always the big blonde," she said, pretending outrage, but laughing in spite of herself.

"Don't worry," Sam said, closing his eyes again, "you're still the most beautiful girl in Diablo. And the only one I could have married."

Chapter Fifteen

The day after Sabrina went home from the hospital, Sam took Seton to Santa Fe for her delivery. He was a bundle of nerves, though he wasn't about to admit that to his wife. He didn't want to visit his worries on her; he wanted her to feel he had everything under control.

Nothing was under control.

Or at least, it didn't feel as if it was. The usually steady, sure Sam in the courtroom was definitely Nervous Dad.

But he couldn't say that to Seton. Instead, as they wheeled her into the delivery room, he said, "It's going to be fine."

He nearly hit the floor when they gave her the epidural. And when it was time for Dr. Stewart to make the first incision, Sam definitely went light-headed. Still, he snapped photos and comforted Seton, making sure he stayed out of the way of the army of nurses and doctors around her.

When the first baby came out, tears welled up so fast Sam felt like Niagara Falls. He snapped pictures, then went over to push Seton's hair back from her face. "She's beautiful. You're beautiful."

A wan smile curved Seton's lips. "Just tell me she's healthy."

He didn't know. They wouldn't know for a while. He said, "She looks great to me, but I'm just the photographer."

He was barely prepared when the second little girl came out. Reality hit him hard. "We have another girl! And she's beautiful, too!"

He watched the neonatal nurses as they carefully cleaned his children and put on breathing tubes, weighed them, checked Apgar something-or-others— that part was beyond him. "For little bitty things, they yell as loud as my brothers," he told Seton, bragging. "Surely that's a good sign."

"They've got the Callahan spirit," she said, and he nodded.

It wasn't long before the third baby was born, and Sam had to take a deep breath to clear his head. He really was going to be a dad to four little girls. The most astonishing thing was happening to him—to Seton and him—and it was magical and wonderful, and he couldn't believe how blessed he was.

It seemed like forever before the fourth baby came out. "Oops," Dr. Stewart said. "This one was a shy one. He was keeping a little secret from us."

"What?" Sam and Seton said together.

"What?" Sam repeated. He went closer to look at the small bundle the doctor was handing off to the neonatal nurses. "It's a boy?"

"It is a boy," Dr. Stewart said. "All boy, I might add."

Tears hit Sam all over again. He had three girls and a son, thanks to Seton. He was certain it was against protocol, but he couldn't stop himself—he went right over and kissed his wife on the lips. "Thank you," he said. "You've just given me everything I never had."

Seton smiled but didn't say anything. But he could see the joy in her eyes. He left her for a moment to check on his children. "How are they?" he asked the nurses. "Besides loud and opinionated, I mean?"

"Small, but steady. About two and a half pounds each, but strong," a nurse told him. He could barely pay attention to what she was saying. His gaze went from baby to baby, trying to take it all in. It was astonishing and amazing that these children were his.

He had his own family now.

And if Seton thought she was getting a divorce, she was in for a surprise. He knew what she was thinking, and he'd always planned to honor their original agreement.

But he could win her over.

At least he hoped he could.

"WITHOUT WEARING YOU OUT with details," Sam told Sabrina on the phone, "your sister is fine, and you have three nieces and one nephew. They can all play with Jonas Cavanaugh, although he'll be a lot bigger and stronger than his cousins."

"That's wonderful!" Sabrina exclaimed. "How is Seton?"

"Tired. Beautiful. Happy. At least I think she's happy. She seems quiet, but I'd be quiet if I'd had four children pulled out of my stomach."

"I'm sure you took lots of pictures for me?"

"You bet. That was just about my only role, besides being Chief Worrywart."

"Did someone say Chief?" Seton asked, waking up from her nap.

"I have to go. Your sister just woke up, and hopefully she'll be hungry. The babies will be staying here for a while, but I think I'll be able to bring Seton home in a few days." Sam frowned, not liking the thought of being so far away from his children. "I don't know, that's actually a plan in flux."

"You're an awesome birth coach. Thanks for calling, Sam. And congratulations."

Sabrina hung up and Sam grinned. He went over to see his little wife, who looked strange to him without the mountain of babies in her stomach. The sheet over her body was flat. "How do you feel?"

She shook her head. "I don't know. Like my body doesn't know what happened to it."

"It doesn't." Sam sat in a chair next to her bed. "The kids are down in the nursery, getting all kinds of attention. You'd be surprised at what attention hogs they are."

"No, I wouldn't. They're Callahans."

If Sam smiled any wider, he thought he'd probably split his head. "They're pretty healthy, for being no bigger than small baking potatoes."

"Sam!" The first smile he'd seen on Seton's face stayed for just a moment, then disappeared. "You can't compare your children to potatoes." She looked at him. "Did I hear you say something about Chief?"

"No," Sam said, "what chief?"

"Chief Running Bear?" She glanced toward the door.

"I said I was Chief Worrywart," Sam said, remembering what he'd called himself during his conversation with Sabrina. "How do you know about Chief Running Bear?"

Seton blinked. "You've talked about him before."

"Oh." Sam shrugged. "No, I was just telling Sabrina how worried I'd been."

"I thought you said you weren't worried."

He looked at his wife. "Now that it's all over, I can admit to a smidgen of husbandly concern, fatherly nerves, whatever."

"Glad you're over it." Seton closed her eyes, hoping that the discussion of Chief Running Bear was closed. "I'm going to nap, husband. Try to stay out of trouble, Chief Worrywart."

Sam laughed, and she heard him leave the room. Seton kept her eyes shut, and thought, *that was a close one.*

Sam drove back to Rancho Diablo, hating to leave Seton in the hospital in Santa Fe, but he needed to check on some things at the ranch. Only so much could be done by phone, and he knew that Seton was being well cared for by a great staff and an army of visitors.

He wasn't worried now about anything except possibly Seton herself. She'd grown more quiet around him, though he suspected that had a lot to do with her body's sudden changes. There was a lot she was trying to learn, and he knew she would try to handle everything with her typical attention to detail.

But he still thought she was quiet—too quiet.

He hoped she wasn't thinking about their agreement. Now that Sabrina had delivered her baby, and no Jonas was in sight, Sam really feared that Seton might decide to pull the trigger on the divorce they'd agreed to.

She had the baby she'd wanted, after all—a whole

insta-family of them. Seton was so independent she just might decide to do it.

"I didn't ever get her locked down," Sam muttered to himself as he climbed out of the truck in Rancho Diablo's drive.

"Talking to yourself?" Rafe asked as he went by with a flashlight.

"Are you looking for ghosts?" Sam demanded. "What are you doing out here at midnight with a flashlight?"

"Thought I heard something." Rafe went on, paying more attention to his bogeyman hunting than his brother.

Which figured. Sam headed to the bunkhouse, tossing his duffel and Dopp kit on the leather sofa.

It was so empty in this house without Seton. Sam glanced around, realizing that he needed to shift Seton's command center back to its normal place and tidy up. She wasn't going to want to come home and be reminded of the many, many days she'd spent on this sofa.

He decided he'd do that tomorrow, before he went back to the hospital. Right now it was time for forty winks—or that was the plan until he heard a slight noise in one of the back bedrooms. Very slight, only a rustle, but something.

It could have been Rafe moving around outside with his stupid flashlight. The bunkhouse was always left unlocked, even more so once Seton had taken up residence on the sofa. Because she couldn't get up and down to answer the door, he'd left a sign on it that read "Babies on Board. Please Be Quiet in Case of Sleeping Mother."

Sam crept to the back, toward where he thought he'd heard the sound.

Something landed hard against his back, and Sam

turned, grabbing the intruder and smashing him against the wall. He socked a nose and kneed a gut, all the while trying to stay out of the way of flying fists. Sam aimed for the groin and, hearing a satisfying curse word, dragged his visitor out of the bunkhouse into the dusty driveway. His assailant landed another punch, splitting skin near his eye, and with a roar, Sam leaped on top of the man, pushing him to the ground. They rolled over and over in the driveway, each trying to gain the upper hand, until Sam finally grabbed a handful of hair and bashed his opponent's head as hard as he could against the ground.

His nocturnal visitor finally lay still beneath him, and Sam tried to catch his breath.

"Hey, Sam, what the hell," Rafe said, walking by again with his flashlight. "I'd think a new father wouldn't have the energy to play in the dirt at this hour."

"Ass," Sam growled, "bring that light and your feeble intelligence over this way so I can see what I'm sitting on."

"Holy crap," Rafe said, directing the beam over the man Sam was perched on. "Friend of yours?"

"Never seen him before." Sam glared at the prone stranger. "Get a rope, would you? He's going to be out for only a minute or two, and I don't have the strength to coldcock him again." Nor the knuckles, Sam thought, flexing his hands.

His brothers ran up in a thunder of boots.

"Is it Bode?" Pete demanded.

"No, which is good, because Julie sure would be mad at her husband if it was." Sam got up and let the others do the trussing. "We'd tell her Rafe beat on her pop, to keep me off Julie's bad list."

"No, we wouldn't," Rafe said, dialing a number on his cell phone, which Sam suspected was Sheriff Cartwright's. "A happy man is one who keeps his wife happy. And I do that by playing dice and dominoes with Julie's pop, not beating the tar out of him."

"Say, stranger," Creed said, kicking the man in the ribs lightly enough to get his attention, "wake up and tell us what's on your mind."

"He's not going to talk," Judah said. "He doesn't look much like a easy squealer. Though we could help him loosen up his inhibitions."

Creed gave the man another nudge. "What's on your mind, stranger? Did Bode hire you?"

"Here's the deal, buddy," Sam said, squatting down next to their visitor. "I haven't had much sleep lately, so I'm a little cranky. The sheriff'll be here in five minutes, so if you want us to go easy on you and tell the officer it was probably just a case of mistaken identity, you need to talk fast."

"Interesting," Judah said, "he's wearing combat boots and has army regulation equipment on him."

"So you're a hire," Sam said thoughtfully, "and that means you're not one of Bode's. It also means you're probably looking for something. What are you looking for, friend?"

"Nothing I'm going to tell you about," their visitor said in a growl. "Get *off* me."

"Nah," Sam said, with a not-too-gentle bounce. "You know what I think? I think you've been hanging around here for a while. Now that I recall all the strange things that have happened that we had no explanation for, I'm wondering about you, friend."

"What are you talking about?" Judah demanded.

"Just to name a few things, which we always blamed on Bode," Sam said, "remember the time Pete got beaned with a two-by-four at the barn during the storm? We wrote that off to wind."

"And when I got locked in the basement," Pete reminded them. "Someone destroyed all of Fiona's canned goods looking for something."

"Yeah," Sam said, "and we never did figure out who shot our brother at Rafe's wedding. But now I think it could have been you, trying to scare us off. Maybe send us a message. Was it you, friend?" he asked, peering down into the stranger's face. "I think after all these years, we finally found the ghost of Rancho Diablo."

"Get *off,*" the visitor snarled, and Sam bounced again, a little harder, drawing a poisonous curse.

"What are you looking for?" Judah demanded. "We don't have anything anyone wants, not that it would take you nearly three years to hang around for. That's a long time to wait for something. You smell a little, like you've been living in the canyons."

"Or the cave," Creed said.

They all stared at the intruder.

"It wasn't the cave," Sam mused. "The chief would have known."

"True," Pete said. "That means the canyons. Damned lonely out there." He shook his head and placed a boot on some unluckily splayed fingers, grinding just a bit. "No girlfriend out there, and minimal food to be found. That makes you a survivor, a hard-ass. Military-trained in survival. What're you after, friend?"

Their nocturnal companion spit, and Sam shook his head. "No one would know if we did him in and buried him in the canyons."

"Nope," Judah said. "Not a soul would know. Obviously, no one would miss him."

"Buzzard bait," Pete stated. "Those little winged devils get hungry, too."

"Count me in," Creed said. "I know the perfect spot for him."

"I'm looking for the Callahans, you sick sons of—"

"Uh-uh," Sam interrupted. "There are ladies on this property, and they *always* have soap nearby. So keep your mouth sweet and clean."

"Do you mean our parents?" Judah asked. "We don't know anything about them."

"They'll come back sooner or later. Sooner, I'd guess," the stranger said, "since someone in that bunkhouse has been trying to find them. Even trying to communicate with them."

"Come back?" Pete said. "Not from the dead, friend, in case you haven't heard."

"They're not dead." The stranger spit again into the dirt. "You jerk, I think you knocked one of my teeth out."

"Sorry," Sam said. "No one in that bunkhouse has been trying to communicate with our parents…."

His words trailed off. A sick feeling crept into Sam's gut. Seton could have. He'd put her on the case in the beginning, to find out who he really was. To alleviate the boredom of her pregnancy, he'd bought her the latest devices, so she could download books, music, puzzles, games, whatever. She had everything she needed to keep searching—including her own laptop.

She could have done a lot of researching in the many days she'd been on the sofa. Her curious mind probably gnawed at her to find out what he and his brothers had never wanted to question.

"Hey," he said to the man he kept pinned to the ground, "if they're alive, why wouldn't they be here? With their family? And home? And grandchildren? Why would you be looking for them? They've been gone for years now."

"They're in witness protection," the stranger said, then cursed.

Sam's insides went totally cold. He glanced around at his brothers. In the light from Rafe's single flashlight, they all wore shocked, haunted, disbelieving frowns.

"That's quite the tale," Sam said, returning his attention to the visitor. "Why would they be in witness protection?"

"Because they were spies. Molly met Jeremiah when she came over from Ireland. They both had similar interests. Molly became a citizen, and as her family had been fighters for the cause in Ireland, she thought nothing of getting involved with Jeremiah Callahan's interest, which was code breaking. They were involved in a situation that went badly wrong, and their identities were leaked. They had no choice but to accept witness protection. But they'll be back," the intruder said. "It's been a lot of years. They'll figure the trail will be cold. They have family to lure them back. And I'll be waiting."

"No, you won't," Sam said. "I'll probably bury you in a cave somewhere, with your boots pointing to hell."

"They'll send someone else."

Sam grunted. "Whoever hired you is wasting their time and money. There's nothing here except our families. We're not even sure we believe you about our parents being alive."

"I don't care. Now get off!"

Sheriff Cartwright pulled up and got out of his truck just then, coming over to check out the prisoner. "I haven't seen him before. Who did the work on him?"

"He came like that," Sam said, and walked away.

"Hey! You said you'd set me free if I talked!" the hire yelled after him.

"Tough luck, that," Sam called back, without turning around.

His wife kept a lot of secrets. He'd always suspected that. But now she'd been in danger, and she hadn't even known it.

There was nothing in this bunkhouse the man could have found. Nothing of interest that proved his story. Everyone knew that the Callahan brothers' parents had been gone for years; the man could have heard that anywhere. There was no reason at all to believe he was telling the truth.

Sam's gaze traveled over the sofa where Seton had been, and her laptop and other devices. Blankets, knitted booties, other projects to keep her busy. And then he saw something poking out from the sofa.

Slowly, Sam pulled out a small journal, written in Seton's clear hand. And after a long moment of wrestling with his conscience, he took a fast peek at the first notation.

Callahan family, early 1940s: Molly Cavanaugh trip from Ireland, settled in Diablo after meeting and marrying Jeremiah Running Bear. Molly and Jeremiah immediately took the name Callahan to

separate from and protect the tribe and Cavana-
ugh family in Ireland. Cavanaugh family unhappy
Molly married Native American spy in America;
disowned; Callahan name history unknown, pre-
sumably maternal relation. Fiona assumed Calla-
han name so nephews wouldn't trace Cavanaugh
family tree and learn she was mother's sister—
not father's sister—to protect their relationship
to tribe. Boys never knew father's surname was
Running Bear. Verbal confirmation from Aunt
Corinne; courthouse records unclear.

Sam read on, more curious about his family history
than anything.

Twenty minutes later, he knew everything about
his wife he hadn't known for the past five and a half
months—including that she did, in fact, believe Molly
and Jeremiah were still alive.

And she had been trying to find them.

But she'd never said a word.

Chapter Sixteen

Sam was quiet, so quiet that it worried her. Seton couldn't escape the nagging feeling something wasn't quite right with her husband, that something was off between them. He still seemed delighted with the babies, but he was very, very careful around her. As if he were walking on china.

There was no more kissing of her fingertips, or teasing about her body. When they chose names for the children, Sam basically let her have all the say, barely offering any suggestions.

"Samuel Jeremiah Bear Callahan," he said for their son.

Seton hesitated, surprised. "And the girls?"

"I'm not so good with girl names." Sam looked perplexed. "Beyond the basic Amy and Susan, I don't know much about girls."

Seton didn't think that was absolutely the truth, but she let it slide. "How about Jennifer Michelle, Julie Marie and—"

"Too many matching monograms. When the girls take off traveling on volleyball or cheerleading trips, or even rodeo, they'll grab each other's bag by accident, and then tears will break out." Sam shook his head. "I say we go for nontraditional and varied monograms."

"You never had any sisters. What do you know about squabbling girls?"

Sam shrugged. "It's just a sixth sense I have. I like to keep confusion to a minimum. It's the organizer in me."

"I'll say." Seton chewed on a pen and considered her husband. "Give me some ideas."

He blew out a breath. "I'm really no good with this. But I like the names Sherry, Blair, Mary and Devon. I don't know why, so don't ask."

She smiled. "Did you ever date any Sherry-Blair-Mary-Devons?"

He shook his head. "I also, strangely, like Bridget."

"All right." Seton looked at her paper, then back at Sam. "How about Mary Sharon and Bridget Devon?"

"She'll hate being called by her middle name," Sam said, clearly worried about his daughters being annoyed with him.

"So maybe Sharon Marie and Devon Bridget?"
Sam nodded. "Maybe."

"And then the littlest one will be—"

"Sarah Colleen," Sam said.

"Perfect," Seton said. "Why didn't we do this sooner?"
"I don't know."

Sam looked out the window, his attention far removed once again, as if he'd completely disconnected from her. Seton shivered, put her pen and pad down and closed her eyes.

"You like to keep notes, don't you?" he asked suddenly.

Seton's eyes snapped open. "I guess so. I've never

really thought about it before. But I am a list girl. I got in the habit of writing things down a long time ago, and it's stayed with me."

"Probably helpful in your line of work."

Seton looked at him. "I suppose so." She thought about his strange mood and his comments for a moment, then said, "Sam, is something wrong?"

He glanced at her, then back out the window. "Everything is fine."

Everything was not fine. She knew it. Something had gone horribly wrong. He'd been so romantic, so perfect, so happy before the babies' birth.

But now he was a different man, one she didn't know.

Seton shivered again.

LITTLE BY LITTLE, the babies gained weight and strength. Seton, too, got stronger. Sam rented a hotel suite in Santa Fe, not too far from the hospital, and when the doctors were ready to release Seton, he moved her there.

"This is wonderful, Sam. Thank you."

Seton turned to him with a smile on her face. Sam had known she wouldn't be able to bear being in Diablo while her babies were here. He wouldn't have, either. So this was the next-best option. He got two beds, one for himself, one for her, telling himself she needed a bed to herself. With all those stitches in her, he didn't want to accidentally bump her in the night.

He'd be too terrified of hurting her.

Seton looked at the two queen-size beds in the room, hesitated for just a moment as if she might say something, then quietly put her overnight bag on the suitcase holder at the end of the bed nearest the bathroom. Sam went and sat on the other bed, pulling off his boots. He flung himself across the duvet and closed his eyes.

"Sam?"

"Yeah?" He didn't open his eyes. Instead, he pulled the pillow under his head, thinking he was pretty smart to get a big enough room for Seton to be able to relax in. It wasn't quite the honeymoon he'd had in mind for when she recovered from her pregnancy and birth and new motherhood, but for now, he hoped it cheered her up.

"Nothing," she said after a moment.

Sam's eyelids seemed as if someone was sitting on them. He felt the warm air kick on in the room, and wondered if they'd be able to bring all four babies home by Christmas.

He hoped so. Christmas was a time for family, and he wanted his family at Rancho Diablo, where they belonged.

"Seton?"

She opened her eyes and looked across at the other bed and Sam. She was more hurt than she would have admitted that he'd chosen to have two beds in their hotel room. On the other hand, she realized he was trying to be considerate.

She missed sleeping with her husband, though. It had been *months*. "Yes, Sam?"

"I've been thinking about your line of work. You're probably going to want to keep working, aren't you? Not now, obviously, but maybe in a year or so?"

"I might. First I'll see how it goes with the babies. They come first."

"Good." Sam was quiet for a moment. "As a private investigator, isn't your job usually revealing things?"

"I guess so. I never thought of it that way." Seton rolled her head so she could see him better. "Why?"

"I've always thought of you as kind of a reserved person. You seem to keep a lot to yourself."

Seton looked away, wondering where he was going with his thought. "My clients have been happy with my work."

"Not me."

Sam rose up on one elbow, and Seton knew he wanted her to look at him. Slowly, she turned her head to face him.

"Did you tell me everything you learned about me?"

"All I really learned was that you are Molly and Jeremiah's son. Then you told me to stop trying to find out any more, and rest."

"And did you?"

Seton swallowed. "Sam, was there something else you wanted to know?"

"Would you tell me if I did?"

Seton's throat dried out. She thought about Chief Running Bear's warning that dire consequences could come of revealing too much, too soon. It wasn't her place to do so, anyway. "I'm not exactly certain what you want me to say, and you seem upset about something."

"You just seem to keep a lot to yourself. I wouldn't say you're exactly secretive, Seton, but sometimes that's the word that fits."

"What happened, Sam? Why are you asking me all these questions?" Seton was truly confused. "I think you know I just spent the last five and a half months having morning sickness and being glued to the sofa. It's been a matter of survival some days."

He looked at her for a long time, then rolled back onto his pillow. "Okay."

The word had a note of resignation in it, as did his voice. She felt him withdraw from her. "Sam, I don't understand, I really don't. Are you upset about something?"

"No," he said, but his tone was clipped. "Let me know if you need anything, all right?"

"Thank you," she said, and Sam rolled onto his side facing the opposite wall.

They might be in the same room, but Seton was brutally aware that she was sleeping alone.

It was a great relief to Sam a couple weeks later when the bellybutton IVs were removed from his babies and PICC lines for feeding inserted. Though it sounded painful to have tubes in their arms, Sam knew his babies were getting the nutrients they needed to grow, and with each of them weighing just over two pounds, he wanted them to get all the help they needed. Soon they would be able to try some breast milk, to see if they could digest it, and Seton had been pumping milk like mad. All this felt like good progress to Sam, and if it wasn't for the tension between him and his wife, he'd be the happiest man on the planet.

But there *was* tension. He could tell that Seton was upset about something, but he decided to write it off to hormones and bodily changes. She'd been through an awful lot, and no doubt her body was trying to readjust. Just the ups and downs of her blood pressure had been an ordeal for her, when she was used to being active and healthy. He considered buying her a present, then discarded the idea. The only thing she'd ever wanted was a child, and no gift he bought her could change the fact that she had everything she needed.

For now, they both had everything they'd wanted. He'd been seeking knowledge, and she'd yearned for a baby.

He figured they could call their business arrangement a success. In spite of everything he knew and yet didn't know about his wife, despite the suspicion he had about the book she'd hidden in the sofa, he was in love with Seton.

He just didn't know what to do about it. Falling in love had not been part of their bargain.

Maybe it was best to say as little as possible, and hope that time was the great healer.

GRADUALLY, the babies proved they could gain enough weight, feed well enough and breathe on their own all the time, and began to go home. Sam Bear was home by Christmas. Though he was born last, he grew the most quickly. Sam told Seton that Bear decided to be strongest so he could protect his sisters later on. Seton had said Bear was probably a typical Callahan male, eager to hit the road.

Sam figured that was probably true of the Callahans—except for him. In spite of his earlier stated goal to go fly-fishing in Alaska or hitting the Amazon, he felt remarkably homebound.

Seton agreed and kissed him on the cheek.

It was a start.

Two weeks after that, little Sherry went home. She'd plumped up nicely to over six pounds. Sam remarked to

Seton that maybe this one was eager to ring in the New Year at the ranch, and Seton said their daughter wasn't the only one.

The following week, Devon hit the road for the ranch, and at that point, Sam told Seton she had to go, too.

"I can't leave little Sarah," she protested. "She doesn't feed well unless I hold her."

"We'll drive in every day," Sam promised.

"Two hours?"

"We can do it," Sam said. "But the other three need their mother, too."

There was no other way to work it, so that's what they did. With the army of volunteers and diaper service and every other kind of aid, Sam hoped his wife would be able to relax sometimes.

Yet with three babies at home, relaxing was nearly impossible. Fortunately, they had sisters-in-law—and brothers—with a lot of experience. Sam found himself running his own diaper-and-bottle rodeo with the babies, and still felt they weren't covering all the bases.

He figured Seton had to be exhausted.

Finally, in late January, Sarah Colleen decided she missed her brother and sisters so much that she convinced the doctors and nurses she, too, was ready to head to Rancho Diablo. Sam and Seton packed her up in the truck, said goodbye to the people who had become their "other" family, and made for home.

The ride was pretty quiet. Sam thought Seton was probably tired—he was whipped himself—so he didn't say much.

When they'd nearly gotten home, Seton finally spoke. "Sam?"

"Yeah?" He didn't take his eyes from the road. Between them, Sarah slept comfortably in her new carrier, positioned backward for safety. It was nice, because he could see her face. Every few moments he'd glance over to check on her, but she never moved, her sweet, shell-shaped eyelids closed in contentment.

"One of your sisters-in-law mentioned that there'd been a slight incident at the ranch, and she thought I should be careful about keeping the bunkhouse door locked when you're not around."

Sam pulled into the drive at Rancho Diablo. "It was no big deal. I wouldn't worry about it. There are so many people in and out of the bunkhouse all day that I know everything is safe as Fort Knox."

He got out of the truck, went around to the other side to help Seton out, then unbuckled Sarah's safety seat. "Home sweet home, beautiful," he told his daughter, and carried her inside.

"Hi," Corinne said, standing when they walked in with the new arrival. "Oh, isn't she an angel!"

"She's the littlest angel," Sam said proudly, "but she's a survivor."

"Of course she is." Corinne looked at Seton. "Do you want me to stay? The babies are taking their naps. I'm happy to watch them, but I wonder if you would like time to settle in as a new family of six."

Seton nodded. "Thank you, Aunt Corinne. I think we could use some time to digest being all together for the first time."

"Then I'll be off." Corinne picked up her purse and took one last look at Sarah as Sam lifted her from the car seat and held her against his chest. "Oh, that one's going to be a daddy's girl. Bye, you two!"

She went out, closing the door behind her. Sam and

Seton sank onto the sofa, with Sarah still happily cuddled against her father's chest.

"I can hardly believe it," Seton said. "We're finally all in one place!"

Sam closed his eyes. "Amazing how one begins to appreciate the small things." He kept his hand on Sarah's back, bracing her so she'd feel protected. "You're a really small thing, Sarah Colleen, and we really appreciate you. We're certainly glad that you decided to join us."

"She's a doll," Seton said. "I think she looks like you."

"Don't say that," Sam said wryly. "I'm hoping she'll look like her mother."

"They're all dark-haired like you."

"The nurses said that a lot of babies are born with dark hair and it sometimes comes in lighter later on. I'm hoping for a blonde or two. I like blondes," Sam said, feeling cheerier just thinking about the possibility of more blondes in his life.

"Sam, why didn't you tell me about the incident?" Seton said, and he sighed.

"It wasn't important, honestly, Seton. You're safe here."

"I'm not worried about me," Seton said. "I'm worried about you."

He heard what sounded like tears starting in her voice, and turned to look at her. "Why would you do that?"

"Because Julie said you got into a fight with some vagrant." Seton gave him a look guaranteed to make him feel guilty. It worked pretty well, too, as a feeling of remorse slid through him.

"It wasn't really a fight," Sam said. "Trust me, I've been in fights. It was more like a sit-down with a new acquaintance."

"Sam!"

"Oh, hell," he said, wishing Julie had kept her judge mouth closed. Julie was right to be cautious and warn Seton about keeping the door locked, Sam knew, but right now, he was tired. Actually, he wasn't so much tired as into avoidance. He simply hadn't wanted Seton to know.

It was a conversation he'd planned to have another day, another time.

"Seton, it was no big deal. You've had a lot to handle. It wasn't important enough to bring up."

"You don't think that some thug on our property attacking you isn't important enough to bring up?" She sounded annoyed as hell now, and the way she'd outlined her question, Sam couldn't blame her.

"Look, it just didn't rise to my radar screen with all the running back and forth to Santa Fe. Primarily, my attention has been on the five of you."

Seton stared at him. "Or ranch matters are not my concern."

"No, it's not that." Sam saw that they were heading into deep, troubled waters, and tried to steady the boat. "My main thought that night was how glad I was that you weren't the one who came home to find him."

"Find him?" Seton asked.

"Yeah." Sam shrugged. "Better me than you. Although I wouldn't go against you in a brawl, sweetie. After watching you have these babies, I know how tough you are."

She wasn't mollified. "How could I have found him? Where was this vagrant?"

Sam swallowed, realizing he'd made two errors. One, Julie had told Seton it was merely a vagrant who'd been on the property. Maybe that's what Rafe had told Julie; Sam didn't know. Since Seton had been the one who'd unwittingly brought the hired gun to the house with her digging around in Sam's family tree, he hadn't wanted to bring it up at all.

Second mistake: Julie hadn't told Seton the man was in the bunkhouse and had attacked Sam in this very room. His throat tightened a bit more. Likely his sister-in-law had glossed over the facts, in order to avoid worrying Seton to death. Julie had probably said something like, "The guys found some idiot on the property, and Sam chased him off, but for safety's sake, you might want to keep the bunkhouse locked when just you and the babies are home."

He looked at Seton. "What exactly did Julie tell you, honey?"

She shook her head. "I'd rather hear about this from you, thanks. I'm well aware of your ability to edge facts to fit the puzzle, Counselor."

"Nuts," Sam said with a sigh. "All right." He glanced around at all four babies, but they were sleeping peacefully and disinclined to throw him a rope. Why was it they couldn't poop or need a soothing bottle of breast milk—better yet, a breast—when he needed them to? "Seton, I surprised the guy in this room. Or actually, in the back of the house. I think he might have been either in the nursery or—"

"In here! And you weren't going to tell me someone had broken into the bunkhouse?" His wife glared at him.

"I would have one day." That much was the truth. He'd just wanted to open the conversation about the notebook he'd found and the hire all at one time, since they were related topics. He had the logical mind of a lawyer, but right now, his wife's extralogical mind was lining up facts that weren't in his favor. "Seton, what was I supposed to do? Scare the hell out of you?"

"Like I wasn't scared when Julie said you'd been in a fight?"

He shrugged. "As I said, it really was more of a heated conversation."

"Julie said the man was lucky you didn't twist his head off." Seton stated that fact not with pride, but with obvious disapproval of his version of the story.

"Yeah," Sam said with a weak smile. "Your husband's got a short fuse at times. Guess I didn't disclose that up front, huh?"

She shot him an annoyed look. "You could have been hurt!"

"Oh, come on, Seton, I'm not a pansy. I can handle one—"

She reached for one of her infernal lists, which he saw she'd tucked into Sarah's diaper bag. "Military. Around six foot one. One-eighty. Operative." Seton looked at him. "Those were a few of the facts I got from Sheriff Cartwright when I inquired about the incident you and Julie were clearly playing down." Seton gave him another accusing look when Sam didn't deny anything. "Sam! You're a lawyer. You don't lift anything heavier than a saddle. You've been a couch potato with me for the past four or five months. What would give you the idea you could take on some kind of military ex-commando?"

"Adrenaline. Anger. I didn't think about it, to be honest. Rage pretty much ruled my head at that moment. He was in my house where my wife had been. Besides which," Sam said, perking up as he remembered the fight, "I have five brothers. Don't count me out, gorgeous. We grew up beating the hell out of each other. Boys use battles to determine the pecking order. And I wasn't much on getting pecked. Now Jonas, he was the lightweight. But I was the youngest, so I—"

Seton cut off his bragging with an impatient wave. "There will be no fighting in our home. I hope you understand that, Sam."

"I would never fight with you, Seton," Sam said, alarmed that she would even think he might have a violent tendency with her.

"I know that! I meant with Bear! You are *not* to teach him to fight." Seton glared at him. "There will be a hands-off rule, and you will tell Bear that he is never to put his hands on another human in anger."

"But Seton—"

"No," she said. "Absolutely no fighting."

"You don't understand," Sam said. "It's a communication thing with boys. It determines their whole lives. I'm not saying they should be violent people, I'm saying that if we hadn't wisely adjudicated our battles, we would have been the town sissies. And you have no idea what a curse that would be," he said, shaking his head. "Even the biggest poindexter in our clan could throw a decent punch. That would be Jonas, in case you couldn't figure it out," he said, looking at Seton with hope for forgiveness in his eyes.

She shook her head. "Bear will not fight. There will be no schoolyard brawls."

Sam sighed. "That leaves his sisters to defend him. The Callahan name will go down in flames."

Seton rolled her eyes. "You're incorrigible."

Probably he was. Sam decided to shelve the topic for another day.

"What I couldn't get out of the sheriff was what the man was after. And did you have to hurt him?" Seton demanded, returning to the subject. "Sheriff Cartwright said your victim had to have a tooth put back in and a few stitches!"

Sam sighed. "Seton, I hardly got warmed up before he went down, I promise."

"Julie says you threatened to bury him in a cave with his toes pointing to hell."

"Damn it!" Sam glared at Seton. "Does Julie just sit in here and gossip with you?"

"It's not gossip if it involves my husband," Seton said airily. "What did he want, anyway?"

"He wants," Sam said, goaded into being more open than he intended, "to kill our parents, who apparently are still alive, a fact you might know something about." He stared at Seton, watching her eyes widen as his words sunk in. "So, my love, contrary to me being the secret-keeper in the family, I believe that title goes to you."

Chapter Seventeen

Seton felt herself go pale. *Secret-keeper*. That was what Running Bear had called her. She stared into Sam's angry eyes, which normally gazed at her with such kindness, and realized there was more he'd been keeping from her besides the fact that he'd played a bit rough with an assailant he'd surprised in the bunkhouse.

"Sam," she said, watching his big palm circle little Sarah's back in comforting motions, "I don't know anything about your parents except that they might not have died the way you were told."

"But your notebook I found lodged in the sofa tells a different story," he said softly, and realization hit Seton.

"If you read my journal, you know I have little more information than I'd already given you." She blinked. "I'm sorry I didn't tell you, Sam, but there were reasons I didn't."

"Well, just as you would have liked me to tell you that there was an ex-militia hire on the property, I would have liked you to tell me what you'd learned about my parents. I would have preferred you to be in here resting, as I thought you were, sweetheart, instead of digging like a squirrel in a garden. But I believe that didn't happen."

"I'm sorry, Sam. I shouldn't have." Now she knew what had been bothering her husband for the past couple of months. She remembered him asking her about her love of lists—though she hadn't realized he'd read her notes on their family. "I wanted you to know. I wanted you to have peace, Sam. But then Chief Running Bear came, and he told me he knew what I'd found, but that I couldn't tell you or anyone because dire consequences could result." Seton looked at Sam, seeing nothing but disappointment and disbelief in his eyes.

"Running Bear knew, too?" Sam glanced around the room. "That means the place is being bugged. Or something. Because the commando knew you'd been contacting someone about our family."

Seton felt the blood rush from her face and her blood pressure drop, just as it had in the hospital after she'd given birth.

Only this time the light-headed, weak feeling was due to shock.

"Are you saying your attacker came here because of something I did?"

Sam nodded, his gaze narrowed as he looked around the room. "That's exactly what I'm saying. You're the only one who was in this bunkhouse actively seeking out information about our parents."

She shook her head, agonized. "I would never have purposefully brought danger to Rancho Diablo, Sam."

"You didn't know the history—nor did I," Sam said, and Seton was grateful he acknowledged that. "How could Running Bear have known? Who were you talking to? Or emailing?"

Seton blinked. "Aunt Corinne. The library. I checked some courthouse files. I think that's all."

"Nothing military?"

She shook her head. "I have no access whatsoever to anyone in the military."

Sam closed his eyes, still rubbing Sarah's back with his hand. It dawned on Seton that he was going to be a great father. He loved his children. Somewhere between *I don't want any* and *maybe one would be all right,* Sam had become a father who truly loved his small offspring.

With a sinking heart, Seton realized that he might not ever be able to love her, not after all the secrets she'd kept. But he was every inch a good and loving father.

Her heart broke. This was her own fault. She'd asked an awful lot of their marriage. Maybe not everything was her doing, but she thought it would be difficult for Sam to believe the best of her.

She hadn't meant to hurt him.

"I am so sorry," she said again, knowing that her apology couldn't really make up for what she'd unwittingly stirred up.

"I know," Sam said. "So am I."

He closed his eyes again.

The discussion was over.

IN THE NEXT SEVERAL DAYS, they were too busy to talk. The babies needed attention all the time, and Seton and Sam took two weeks with everyone out of the house, to see how much they could handle on their own. Sam ran the pediatrician routes, and Seton did a lot of breast-feeding for the ones who wanted it, and bottle feeding for the babies who weren't inclined to wait their turn.

It was the most hectic time of Seton's life, but she loved every minute. Except for the distance between her and Sam, everything was perfect.

Being a mother was just as wonderful as she'd ever imagined it could be.

"You're flourishing," Sabrina said when she came to visit, and Seton smiled.

"Not flourishing. But I would say we're getting the hang of it."

"How does Sam feel about being a dad?"

Seton picked up Bear and checked his diaper before settling him in her lap. "He loves that part."

"And everything else?"

"We're too busy to think of anything beyond survival at the moment," Seton answered, trying to avoid her sister's question.

"I've decided to stay in Diablo," Sabrina said, changing the subject, for which Seton was grateful. "As much as I loved living in D.C., I love living here with family more. It'll be nice for my son to have cousins to play with."

"I'm so glad you're staying." Seton had hoped that was a decision Sabrina would make, but she also understood it might be awkward for her sister here. "I'd miss you so very much if you went back."

"Well, I'm going to have to go back for a bit, to pack up my stuff and clean out my apartment. And I need to find a place here. Aunt Corinne says I can keep using the upstairs bedroom, but I worry I'd be disrupting her life too much. She's not used to having an infant around."

Seton smiled at that. "I don't think Aunt Corinne is too worried about babies disrupting her life. She's over here all the time."

"I know." Sabrina smiled down at her son, Jonas Cavanaugh McKinley who lay quietly in his carrier. "Mom and Dad are dying to come visit."

"I know. I don't think we can hold them off much longer. The only thing that's kept them away is the fact that I wasn't supposed to have visitors, and they wanted to see all the babies at once." Seton looked at her sister. "I get why you named your baby Jonas, although it's a dead giveaway, even for Big Jonas, when he returns—"

"No. I call the baby Joe," Sabrina said. "Jonas will never know, at least not until I decide to tell him."

"So what's with the Cavanaugh?"

Sabrina thought about it for a minute. "It was Jonas's mother's maiden name."

Seton hesitated. "How did you find that out?"

"I looked up their family tree online. It's not hard," Sabrina said. "I was thinking about baby names, and when you were resting one day, I used your laptop to see what I could find. I hope that was all right."

"I don't mind at all," Seton said. They'd always shared each other's things, anyway. "What did you find?"

Sabrina shrugged. "I put in Callahan, Rancho Diablo, and Fiona's name, and I turned up Cavanaugh. Funny, because I always thought that Jeremiah was Fiona's brother. But it turns out Fiona was Molly's sister. I guess I had that wrong."

"I think a lot of people did," Seton said softly. "And then what?"

"I put in Ireland, and Cavanaugh came up. Molly and Fiona Cavanaugh were born in Dublin."

Sabrina had easily found a lot of the same information she had. Seton glanced at her laptop, thinking about Running Bear knowing that she was searching, and also

Sam claiming the intruder had known that she was actively trying to find out more about their parents.

"Sabrina, do you ever get those flashes of intuition anymore?"

"Clairvoyance?" She shrugged. "Sometimes. Not as much as I used to. I think I'm too tired from being a new mom. I'm not getting much sleep. More than you are, but not as much as before. Or maybe I'm just not as in tune to it now that I have little Joe to focus on." She smiled proudly at her round, happy baby.

Seton looked at her sister. "Would you know if there was a presence on this ranch that didn't belong here?"

"You mean that no one else knew about?" Sabrina shook her head. "I don't think so. Not unless it came to me. I never know when it will happen. Sometimes when I shake someone's hand, I can tell in that moment if that person is good, or not feeling well, things like that. But I haven't felt anything at Rancho Diablo that isn't right. I never even got bad feelings about Bode, and the Callahans were certain he was the devil."

Seton didn't think the Callahan parents were at the ranch, hidden away as Sam's attacker had supposedly been. Someone would have noticed two people living in the canyons....

She sighed. "My mind is going crazy."

"Lack of sleep." Sabrina stood, picked up Joe's carrier. "I'm going to go. Try to get some rest."

"I'll try. You, too. Bye, baby Joe." Seton watched her sister walk out the door, then moved to her laptop.

And then it hit her: it was all the searching she and Sabrina were doing. If the intruder had made it into the bunkhouse once, he'd probably done it before. And her laptop had always been out, sitting on the coffee table or in the office, easily accessible to Sabrina—or anyone else.

Seton searched through her computer, looking for recently uploaded files, then checked the programs and ran a spyware scan.

After hunting for five minutes, she turned up what she'd been looking for: a data-mining bug had been installed on her laptop.

Someone had known, every time she'd searched, what she'd been looking for and what information she'd turned up. Her investigative skills had given her many of the answers she'd been seeking—and they'd also let someone else know the same information.

She could have led the bad guys right to Sam's parents, wherever they were, if they were still alive. Whoever he was, he'd bided his time, letting her do all the work.

She'd brought danger to Rancho Diablo—just as Running Bear had tried to warn her.

Chapter Eighteen

"So tell me how you figured out it was the laptop?" Sam asked Seton the next day, when she decided it was time to clear her conscience. The knowledge of what she'd done had kept her up all night. She'd been up anyway, with Sarah Colleen's colic and Bear's unsettled cries because his sister was upset. But Seton's mind hadn't been able to rest, thinking about what could have happened to Sam.

That was what tortured her the most. What if he'd been hurt? Sam's attacker had the element of surprise on his side. In spite of all her tough talk about Sam not letting Bear fight, she was secretly very glad her husband had been able to defend himself.

The thought that she could have lost Sam had nearly given her a nervous fit. While the babies always calmed her down—she loved being with them, no matter the time of day or night—last night she'd been jangled, jumpy, unable to tell Sam how she really felt.

Now she looked into his denim-colored eyes and told herself how lucky she was that everything had turned out all right. "Sabrina said she used my laptop one day while I was napping. That made me realize that my computer was always out and always available. And if your attacker had gotten in here once, he'd probably found it very easy to do so on other occasions. Most likely in the early morning, when it was still dark outside and you'd gone to work." Seton shivered. "Sometimes I slept pretty hard when I was pregnant."

"I guess that makes sense, though I don't like the thought of someone breaking in while you were here."

"I know. It's creepy." Seton looked around at the four Moses baskets holding the babies in the common room and shrugged. "No one could come in and surprise us now. Someone is always awake in this house."

Sam nodded. "True. Go on."

"So I scanned my computer and finally turned up a tracking bug. I think you should take the computer to Sheriff Cartwright and let his people look it over. He probably knows the right place to have it checked thoroughly, for bugs and any other evidence that could help him."

"But you have all your personal and work files on there."

Seton shrugged. "Nothing that Mr. Ex-Commando hasn't already seen. And as far as clients, I don't keep their information on my laptop for just that reason. I move everything to separate memory sticks for each client in case I ever lose my laptop or it's stolen. I keep the memory sticks in a lockbox for privacy and safekeeping."

"Good girl," Sam said. "I wouldn't have thought of that."

"So the only thing on there that he could track was where and with whom I was making contact about your family. That was really the only case I was working on at the moment, anyway. Everything else had been swept off."

"I'll take it to the sheriff," Sam said. "They're not going to be able to hold that guy forever. They have to have something to charge him with, and I don't know if breaking and entering is enough. Someone might post bail for him."

"No one will post bail for him," Seton said. "He's been off the radar for years, living in the canyons, waiting on your parents. He's basically a phantom. If you *had* buried him in a cave, no one would have come forward. I doubt he has any family at all. Whoever he works for is the only one who cares about his existence, and even then he's expendable."

Sam looked at her. "You're good at what you do, aren't you? This P.I. stuff?"

"My clients seem happy with the results," Seton said carefully. "I get plenty of referral work."

"Is it dangerous? I don't want you working anymore if what you're doing is dangerous."

"Okay," Seton said, "I'll just sit here in my own house, where people who want to kill your family come in and snoop."

Sam blinked. "You're right. We're going to have to move."

"I didn't say a thing about moving!" Seton was aghast at the conclusion he had drawn.

"I know, but we'll have to. This bunkhouse is way too open and there are too many doors and windows for it to be safe." Sam glanced toward his four sleeping children, who were content to rest for the moment after their busy night of colic and tears. "Anything could happen."

Seton frowned. "Don't you think it's safer here,

where there's a lot of people? That's what your aunt wanted—everybody on the ranch, one big happy family in one big compound. Really, Sam, I think you're jumping the gun."

He shook his head. "You need to be in town. There's a two-story, white brick house—the Stevens' place—that's gone on the market. It's probably six thousand square feet, built in the old style, so every one of these munchkins could have their own bathroom. Well, two of them would have to share, but girls do that all right, don't they?"

"Not always," Seton said. "But Sabrina and I did, and it was fun."

"There you go," Sam said. "I'll go by and look at it tomorrow."

"I don't want to move," Seton protested. "I like the bunkhouse."

"No one raises their family in a bunkhouse, Seton. A long time ago, all the wranglers and hands lived in this place. At least they did until Fiona decided we were old enough to work the ranch ourselves."

"Sam, take the laptop to the sheriff. I want to nap. I don't want to think about intruders and mystery visitors anymore. And I truly don't want to move away from my new sisters. I love it at Rancho Diablo."

Sam picked up the computer. "You sure you'll be all right with the munchkins?"

"Yes, Sam." Seton waved her worrying husband away. "Go. If you hurry, I might get twenty minutes of sleep before they awaken."

"I'm already gone," Sam said, and disappeared.

Seton blew out a breath.

She lay down on the sofa and closed her eyes. Sam

was so handsome and so protective. He was so much more than she'd ever dreamed she'd find in a husband.

The fact that all this craziness had happened because of her was killing her.

TWO WEEKS LATER, Sam came home to the bunkhouse to find an unpleasant surprise: Seton was packing. There were stacks of her clothes and baby paraphernalia laid out on the bed, with more folded in a black suitcase.

It felt as if a knife had been launched at his chest.

"What are you doing?" he asked, holding the bouquet he'd brought for her. Spring flowers he'd bought at the florist shop, which he hoped would put a smile on Seton's face. Lately, she seemed so quiet, so withdrawn.

He was hoping it was because of the babies, and adjusting to their new lifestyle, but the suitcase told a different story.

Seton turned to face him. "Sam, I've been doing a lot of thinking—quite a lot of thinking, actually, and—"

"No," Sam said. "You're not backing out on this deal now, angel cake."

She looked at him for a long moment, then started over. "I think it's for the best, Sam. We got married for such different reasons than what our marriage has turned out to be."

"No one can predict what their marriage is going to be like," Sam said. "And you're not going to weasel out on me now."

She put down the tiny onesies she'd been folding. "Sam, listen. As much as I care about you, I can't get over the fact that I brought a lot of trouble to Rancho Diablo. I'm sure your brothers are wondering why you married someone who drew more worry than anyone else to the family. I know for a fact that all your brothers are totally happy with their wives."

"Yeah, well, don't think their wives don't give them plenty of trouble, because they do. So unpack that damn suitcase, and don't even talk to me about running off. We have four babies counting on us, and we're going to do the right thing by them. So just settle down, Calamity Jane."

Seton shook her head. "Whether you admit it or not, you're not as happy as your brothers are, Sam. You wanted to be footloose and free. You got us instead." She gestured to herself and the babies. "Any man would be entitled to feel resentment over the way I roped you into having children."

"Yeah, well," Sam said, "how about you let me decide what my feelings are? For a brainiac P.I., you don't know as much as you think you do about your husband, which should be the easiest thing you have to consider. How about a little skullduggery with your husband, sweetie?" he asked, handing her the flowers. When she took them from him, he swept her into his arms and kissed her lovingly on the lips.

Seton pulled back after a moment, trying to catch her breath. "Wow, it's been a long time since you kissed me like that."

"I've been trying to give you a break. Now that I know you're getting all restless on me, I'll just have to remind you why you tied me down in the first place."

Seton narrowed her eyes at him. "I didn't do all the tying, cowboy." She laid the flowers on the table, and he thought his gift had pleased her. He pressed on with his suit.

"Still, you're very talented at throwing a rope, Seton.

Caught me in one try." He reached for her, and pulled her toward the bedroom. With any luck, maybe the babies would stay napping for another few minutes, long enough for him to romance his suddenly guilty wife.

Sweeping her up in his arms, he carried her down the hall and dropped her on the bed, where he gave her a light spanking. "Listen, gorgeous, you might have gotten a case of cold feet, but those babies won't be going anywhere. You need a day or two to get some crazy out of your system, fine. But those bundles of joy stay with their daddy."

She jumped off the bed when he released her. "Sam, you can't just pretend to spank me and think that your case is rested."

"You're right. You sidetracked me with your travel plans. Come here, my turtledove, and let me finish the job." He massaged her bottom through her denim dress, and then reached underneath to find bare skin, making certain that she knew how much he wanted her. He kissed her lips, her neck, made his way down to the lacy camisole edging **the** front of her dress. "You're beautiful, Seton."

She didn't say anything. But she wasn't running away.

Sam decided now was an excellent time to remind Seton why she wanted to stay right here with him at Rancho Diablo.

"CONVINCED?" Sam asked Seton about twenty minutes later. He was feeling pretty good about his performance. From his wife's moans and squeals, he thought he'd made her pretty happy.

"For a quickie," Seton said, "yes, I think I am."

"If that was your version of a quickie, we're going to have a long and happy marriage."

Seton smiled. "It's been a long, long time since you've held me, Sam."

"It's been a long, long time since you were available, goddess." Sam rolled up on one elbow and stared down at his beautiful wife. "So there'll be no more talk about you putting on your tennis shoes and doing the cold-feet run."

"You may have changed my mind for the moment," Seton said, stretching. "But if any more of your little friends show up around here, I'm going to hit them with a broom."

"I thought you said we would never be laying hands on anyone in violence in this home."

Seton gave a wry grimace. "I said you weren't to teach Bear to fight."

"That leaves me the girls. Trust me, girls can be just as good fighters as boys. They're meaner."

Seton laughed. "Not my little cupcakes."

"So our bargain is back on." Sam got out of bed, thinking he heard the "cupcakes" starting to move around in their Moses baskets.

"I'll think about it after you get rid of your canyon friend for good." Seton got up, too, and he appreciated her charms as she pulled on her dress.

"He's still in jail. There's nothing to worry about."

"There is," Seton said. "Have you ever wondered what he was surviving on out there?"

Sam shrugged. "I don't care if he was catching snakes and drinking his own p—"

"Sam. There'll be no disgusting talk in this house, either."

He grinned. "What is disgusting to you might be survival to another."

Seton looked at him. "I'm thinking about Aunt Fiona's canned preserves that were destroyed."

Sam zipped his jeans and tried to follow Seton's line of thought. It was hard, because just looking at her getting dressed was making him think about pulling that dress off her again. "So?"

"He might have made it into her basement once, but he wasn't coming onto the ranch often enough to steal leftovers and preserves for survival."

"The canyons aren't far from the next town. He wouldn't have had to come into Diablo for supplies." Although now that Sam thought about it, the man *had* come onto Rancho Diablo several times that they knew of. They'd always blamed the incidents on Bode, but...

"Someone had to have seen him, Sam," Seton said, "and that's what bothers me. He didn't just now get caught because we were lucky. If he installed a tracking device on my laptop that I could find, as little as I know about spyware, there could be more stuff. Which means he had some type of communication device of his own in order to install it. That leads me to think that he is accessing Wi-Fi from a hot spot somewhere."

"It wouldn't take him twenty minutes to walk to Ponce Laredo from the canyons. Banger's has Wi-Fi, but I doubt he would have been that bold." Sam realized that Seton was never going to be able to rest now, not with her mind teasing over the facts they knew about the intruder.

And Sam had to have her focused on the babies, and herself, and him, all the time, if their marriage was going to survive. She needed to rest and heal and enjoy the one thing she'd always wanted: motherhood.

So he said the only thing he knew to say.

"It doesn't matter, Seton. He's locked up. He can't bother us anymore." At least not for a while, Sam thought, walking down the hall to stare at his babies. *If he ever came back in this house, I would personally kill him with my bare hands, regardless of Seton's opinions on the matter.*

Sudden rage made Sam kind of crazy as he realized what he would do to protect his family. He loved these children fiercely; he loved his wife like he'd never loved anyone in his life. "I'll take care of you," he told the babies, and behind him Seton said, "I know, Sam."

He turned to her. "Just don't think about leaving anymore. Go unpack that damn suitcase."

"Try to understand, Sam," she said after a moment. "He would never have been here if it wasn't for me. And I don't know who he might have told. He was informing someone somewhere."

Sam narrowed his eyes, thinking. "You're probably right. I'll have the foremen who live on the outskirts of the ranch, Johnny Donovan and Jagger Knight, keep an eye out."

She took a deep breath, knowing the moment had come. "You might want to talk to Chief Running Bear, too."

Sam looked at her. "He doesn't live on the ranch, Seton. He just appears from time to time."

"He knows about the guy, Sam," Seton said softly. "I know he does, because the chief asked me not to tell you anything until the time was right. I think that time is now."

Sam shook his head. "How much time did you two spend chatting?"

"Not long. Later, I realized that Running Bear had known all along that the man was in the canyons."

The chief would know. He knew every inch of this land. It had been his tribe's before they'd sold it to Jeremiah.

"Is this your last secret?" Sam asked his wife.

"Absolutely," she said. "The rest of our life together will be an open book. I promise."

He looked at her. "I'm not going to talk to the chief. It won't do any good." Sam thought about it, checked his emotions, realized it was true. "Whatever he didn't want us to know, we still don't know. And that's fine."

It was true. For him, it was over. He pulled Seton down next to him on the sofa and glanced over at their babies. "Are we staying in this bunkhouse?"

"I am, if you are," Seton said shyly.

"Good. Because the thing is, I don't need to know any more than I do." As Sam spoke the words, he knew they were true. "I don't care about the chief. I don't care about the hire. I'll let Jonas mop everything else up. Or my other brothers. You did a lot of work, Nancy Drew, but I have a funny feeling that if we look any more into the past, we'll lose sight of the future."

Seton caught her breath. "I want a future with you, Sam."

"Of course you do, love," he said, kissing her fingertips. "I'm the man of your dreams."

"Did you read that in my notebook, too?"

Sam looked surprised. "No. Was it in there?"

She laughed. "No. But it's not a secret, either."

"All right, then. I've got an idea. I think we should

get married again, right here at Rancho Diablo, with no other reason than we want to be together."

Seton hesitated. "Why are you telling me all this now? Is it because I was going to leave?"

"No," Sam said, "you weren't going anywhere. I knew that all along."

Seton smiled at her husband's ego. "So why now?"

"Because you've changed me, Seton. If you go, I'm going to follow you. You're my Alaska, you're my Amazon rain forest. You're my adventure. If I have any more adventure than what you've given me, babe," he said, pointing to the babies, "it'll probably kill me."

She wasn't sure. Could a temporary marriage turn into the real thing? Did he really want her—or just the babies? "There has to be more than that for a marriage to work."

"Not for me. I wanted to find myself. I can keep looking, but the truth is," he said, kissing her on the lips, "I found myself with you and our family. There are a lot of unanswered questions around here, but that's the way it's always going to be. The questions I had about myself are all answered."

Tears flooded Seton's eyes. "Sam, that's so romantic."

"I'm glad you think so." He gave her a long, loving kiss. "But it's not really romantic as much as it is just true. I've loved you for a long time, Seton. I was probably in love with you the first time you and your sister came to our ranch with your silly little game."

"Your aunt hired us," Seton reminded him. "It was very serious to her."

"Fiona is a great lady. I love her dearly. Whatever she knows about us may stay a mystery. You, however, are the only thing I want in life. And these children," he said, gazing down at their babies one more time. "Funny how such small things can change a man."

Seton drew closer to him. "I always wanted a child, Sam. But I want our marriage to work, too. I love having a family with you." She gazed at her husband, full of love and joy that he was hers. "I'll marry you again, if that was a real proposal this time."

Sam got down on one knee, and she held her breath.

"Knowing everything about me that you do, Seton McKinley Callahan, will you marry me at Rancho Diablo, with our family and friends and these wonderful angels you brought into my life?"

Seton smiled and pulled him into her arms. "Sam Callahan, you just got yourself a permanent deal. Yes, I'll marry you."

Sam grinned to himself as he held Seton, and thought that life was perfect. He had his wife, he had his children, and for the rest of his life he was going to be the best father and husband he could manage to be.

Sam Callahan had finally made it home.

Epilogue

The magic wedding gown fit Seton like, well, magic. She felt beautiful wearing the long, exquisitely designed dress that all the Callahan brides wore—and it was true what Jackie, Darla, Aberdeen and Julie had said: she did see the face of the man she loved when she put it on. She did know Sam was the right man for her.

But I knew that, anyway, almost from the first time I ever saw him.

When Sam saw her walking down the aisle between rows of white chairs draped with blue ribbons at Rancho Diablo, his eyes told Seton that he thought she was beautiful, too. And that she was the only one for him.

This was the wedding of her dreams, all that she'd ever hoped for. But it was more than a wedding ceremony; this time it was both of them going into marriage absolutely certain of their love, and of their commitment to each other and their family.

"You look beautiful," Sam said as Seton's father, Max, walked her to his side at the rose-festooned altar. "But then, you always do to me."

Seton smiled at her husband. "I love you, Sam."

"And I love you, babe," he instantly replied.

"Well," Father Dowd said, "this is going to be a remarkably different ceremony than last time, I can tell already!"

The many guests laughed. It seemed everyone had come out to the ranch on this beautiful May day to see Seton and Sam say I do one more time. Seton didn't think she'd ever been happier. Sabrina had agreed to be her maid of honor once again, and Seton just hoped that one day her sister would get the chance to wear the beautiful gown. She glanced at her with a smile, delighted that Sabrina had decided to stay in Diablo permanently.

Better still, their parents were in town for the wedding—and to meet all the new grandchildren. Renee and Max had spent hours with the babies, enjoying being grandparents to the fullest.

It was the most wonderful day of Seton's life.

Well, besides the day she'd had her children. She smiled at Sam as he took her hand, even before the priest asked who would give the bride in marriage. Together Sam and Seton stood at the altar, enjoying the fact that most of their friends and family were there with them.

It would have been perfect if Jonas had been Sam's best man, and if Fiona and Burke had been there to share their joy. But Seton knew that, wherever they were, they would be pleased that Sam and she were so happy together.

And Rafe made an excellent best man, anyway. He was beaming as if it was the first wedding for Sam and Seton, and somehow, she felt that it was.

Sam gently squeezed her hand. "One day you and I will watch our children marry their best friends. Four weddings," he whispered. "That sounds like fun times four to me."

Seton smiled. It was too far in the future to think about. But she was so thankful that the future was theirs, now and forever.

Sam couldn't stop staring at his beautiful wife, and thanking his lucky stars that she was going to be his always. He was so proud that his babies were at the wedding, too. Little Sherry, Devon, Sarah and Bear were in separate carriers, being watched over by doting family and friends, zealously assigned by their very protective great-aunt Corinne. There'd been a lot of sleepless nights, but Sam had enjoyed every single one. He meant what he'd been trying to tell Seton: that she was his best friend. He trusted her with his heart, and he knew she was the woman he'd waited all his life to find. She brought him magic, and total happiness.

He'd been blessed many times over. He was Sam Callahan, husband to Seton McKinley Callahan, and father to four wonderful children.

He was more blessed than he'd ever hoped to dream.

And when Sam suddenly heard the hooves of the mystical Diablos galloping through the deep-hued canyons of Rancho Diablo, he wasn't surprised at all.

* * * * *

HEART & HOME

Harlequin®

American Romance®

COMING NEXT MONTH
AVAILABLE APRIL 10, 2012

#1397 BABY'S FIRST HOMECOMING
Mustang Valley
Cathy McDavid

A year after Sierra Powell gave her baby up for adoption, little Jamie was returned to her. Determined to make a new life for both of them, she returns to Mustang Valley to reunite with her estranged family. But she doesn't expect to run into Clay Duvall, a former enemy of the Powells...and the secret father of her son.

#1398 THE MARSHAL'S PRIZE
Undercover Heroes
Rebecca Winters

#1399 TAMED BY A TEXAN
Hill Country Heroes
Tanya Michaels

#1400 THE BABY DILEMMA
Safe Harbor Medical
Jacqueline Diamond

HARCNM0312